ASKA MOCHIZUKI

Spinning Tropics

Aska Mochizuki was born in Tokyo in 1973. In 1992, after graduating from high school, she found employment at a computer company. But she left the corporate world in 1994 to travel around Australia by bus, taking on a series of part-time jobs (as a shark fisherman's helper and a cleaning woman at a backpacker's hostel, to name just two). She returned home and attended university, graduating in 2002 with a teaching certificate. She embarked immediately for Vietnam to teach Japanese, and returned home to Tokyo in 2004, where she began to write. *Spinning Tropics* was the 2007 winner of the Random House Kodansha Prize.

Wayne P. Lammers is an independent translator and writer who most recently introduced Mitsuyo Kakuta to the English-speaking world with the novel *Woman on the Other Shore*. Besides contemporary Japanese fiction, his work has included a classical romance, memoirs, stage plays, screenplays and subtitles, manga, and a manga-based guide to Japanese grammar. He lives outside Portland, Oregon.

Spinning Tropics

Spinning
Tropics
A NOVEL

Aska Mochizuki

Translated from the Japanese by Wayne P. Lammers

VINTAGE CONTEMPORARIES
Vintage Books
A Division of Random House, Inc.
New York

A Vintage Contemporaries Original, December 2009

English translation copyright © 2009 by Wayne P. Lammers

All rights reserved. Originally published in Japanese as *Kaiten suru nettai* by Random House Kodansha, Tokyo, in 2007. Copyright © 2007 by Aska Mochizuki. First published in the United States by Vintage Books, a division of Random House, Inc., New York, and in Canada by Random House of Canada Limited, Toronto.

Vintage and colophon are registered trademarks and Vintage Contemporaries is a trademark of Random House, Inc.

The Cataloging-in-Publication Data is on file at the Library of Congress.

Vintage ISBN: 978-0-307-47369-1

Book design by Ralph Fowler/rlf design

www.vintagebooks.com

Printed in the United States of America

10 9 8 7 6 5 4 3 2 1

A NOTE ON CURRENCY REFERENCES

The official currency of Vietnam is the dong, but U.S. dollars are in circulation as well, and in many shops prices are shown in both currencies. Since the value of the dong is low—at the time in which this story is set, it was trading at a little over 15,000 dong to the dollar—both expatriates and locals often prefer to use dollars in discussing or buying big ticket items, as the characters in this story do.

Some characters also refer to Japanese yen amounts. The yen was trading near 110 yen to the dollar in the story's time frame.

Spinning Tropics

CHAPTER ONE

THE OVERRIPE CUSTARD APPLE SLIDES from my grasp, slithering out of my hand like an eel making its escape.

"Uh-oh," Hai chuckles, looking down at the piece of fruit on the pavement. Its creamy white flesh is now blackened with dirt and sand. A tangy sweet scent hits my nostrils as I lick my fingers in disappointment.

This little café that Hai runs is on the ground floor of a fifteen-year-old reinforced-concrete apartment building. The café consists of nothing more than a few cheap resin tables and chairs set out at the edge of the street. It's a nice place to relax because it's off the main thoroughfare, a short distance down a quiet side street that gets only occasional traffic. The apartments in the building above have no balconies but large windows. The tenants leave their windows wide open all the time, confident that the iron bars fitted over them will protect them from intruders.

In the morning, along the same side of the street, a variety of food carts offering noodles, rice dishes, and sandwiches set up shop for locals to come fill their empty stomachs. Since so many people make it their custom to buy breakfast from street vendors, this is the time of day when the place most bustles with life. Once the carts have served up their food, they pack up and leave, not to be seen again until the following morning.

Hai's café is the only place that stays open all day long and into the evening. Since it's also a general grocery store, and my apartment is right across the street, I'm a regular. But I've learned to examine things carefully before I buy them. Among the products available in the cluttered, poorly lit storefront are seasonings and canned goods that are a year or two past their expiration dates—and sometimes even more. A pastry I bought once turned out to have a small colony of mold growing on it.

I live across the street in an older building that's supposed to be for Vietnamese citizens only. As a general rule, foreigners in Vietnam can't live anywhere they please; they're required to find housing specifically licensed for non-native occupants. But properties with such licenses charge much higher rents, which is why I live where I do.

My landlord is a quiet middle-aged man who lives with his family on the second floor. On the first floor there's a store that sells baby clothes; the only way for residents to enter the building is through this store. It's never very busy, except during special sales, and I sometimes see the young female salesclerks taking naps in the store's dimly lit interior. They stretch out on the sofa intended for customers or spread reed mats on the floor without the slightest qualm, right in the middle of their shifts.

I often get home after the store closes, so it's dark when I walk through it to my apartment. I could easily steal something if I wanted, but needless to say, I don't. I have no use for baby clothes.

When I come up to the second-floor landing, I peek into the landlord's living room, which is always left wide open. I often used to see his ghostly mother and father standing quietly inside as I passed by. Just once, they beckoned me in and asked me to join them for a cup of tea. Their movements were like those in a slow-motion film. Time seemed to pass even more slowly for them, in their little realm, than for the rest of Vietnam.

The old woman died not too long ago, and the funeral was held in the store downstairs. As is customary, I went to offer up a stick of incense. The man with whom she had shared her life was not present. My heart hurt to think how he must be feeling.

My own apartment is on the fifth floor. I like being on the top floor, where I have a nice view, but the one drawback is that the building has no elevator. The stairwell is dark even in the daytime, and very dusty. Right next to the stairs on the top landing is a messy pile of discarded furni-

ture. When I first moved in, I helped myself to a TV stand
and a chair.

The building has two doormen who work in alternating shifts. The first has a brusque manner that discourages
any attempt at conversation, but the other is an affable fellow who wears milk-bottle glasses. He always seems to be
drinking some kind of cheap booze when he's on night
duty; it looks to me like pretty nasty stuff. When I come
home, he often invites me to join him as I pass by his station.

Behind the store is a small parking lot for bicycles and
motorbikes. The back door leading to the lot has no doorman, so any time I go out that way, I have to make sure
the lock is secure. Given the high incidence of theft here
in Ho Chi Minh City, a momentary lapse could lead to
long-lasting regrets.

The lot isn't really quite big enough for all the two-
wheelers it has to hold, so at night even the center aisle
fills up. If you park at the back and need to get away
early the next morning, you wind up having to do a lot of
shifting—moving the bikes out one by one to open up the
aisle, then putting them all back again after you get your
own bike out. It makes for a whole lot of extra trouble. To
avoid that, you need to be thinking about the next day
when you decide where to park. But unfortunately, if you
park in the spaces closest to the entrance, you're more
likely to get your bike stolen.

Adjacent to the building, right outside the back door, is
a small, dilapidated wooden house where a man who

drives a cyclo—the Vietnamese equivalent of a pedicab—
lives with his family. The structure looks like it could top-
ple over at any moment. I often see the driver waiting for
fares on the corner of the main street; anytime he spots
me coming out the door, heading to the nearby market or
bakery on foot, he immediately calls after me, "Take a
ride, miss?" When he's not out driving his cyclo, I sometimes see him in the alley behind my building, sorting
through mounds of empty tin cans and scrap metal that
he's gathered.

"IT'S ANOTHER HOT ONE, ISN'T IT?"

With friendly smile lines crinkling her face, Hai comes
over to where I'm sitting and repeats the phrase I hear at
least once a day in this city.

"Care for some tea?" she asks, but I shake my head. She
acknowledges with a nod and squats down over a water-
filled bucket beside me to wash some glasses. I watch the
rhythmical movements of her hands for several moments
before looking up at the sky. A few brilliantly white clouds
float in an otherwise clear expanse of blue.

"There she comes," Hai says, gesturing toward the
main street with her chin. I follow her gaze and see Yun
driving up on her silver metallic motorcycle. To my surprise, she's wearing a skirt, and—oh dear!—she has her
legs spread wide open, with her underwear on full display.

"Put your legs together, Yun! Your underwear's showing!"

Yun giggles, paying no attention. "Sorry, I late," she says, in slightly awkward Japanese.

With a cheerful smile, she parks her bike directly in front of my table and sits down beside me.

"As if you're not always late," I snort. "But never mind that. What's this about—you in a skirt? It must be the first time."

"No, not the first time. I wear skirt at wedding, too, of Suong-san."

"Oh, that's right, I remember now. So that makes it the second time."

"Do you like? It's present from sister in Taiwan."

"It's cute. But it's so short, I really don't think you should wear it on your bike." The women in this town think nothing of driving around on motorcycles in stiletto heels and tight miniskirts.

"Okay," she says.

"How's your sister?" I ask.

"She is fine, thank you. She give me presents and money." Yun giggles again.

She is the second youngest of six sisters, two of whom live overseas. One married a man from Taiwan, where she now lives. The other married a fellow Vietnamese but emigrated with him to Australia, where they've built a successful business making and selling furniture. The sister living in Taiwan arrived yesterday on her annual visit home. Both sisters usually return to Vietnam once a year and stay for about a month.

"Together we go to my home later. You already meet my Taiwan sister, yes?"

"Uh-huh. When she was here last year. Her name is Phong, right?"

"Yes, yes. She bring baby, too."

"It's been a whole year, so the baby must have grown a lot. She's two now?"

"She is very cute."

Yun is the sort of energetic person who never stops moving. She's not only full of curiosity, but highly enterprising, ready to take charge and get things done. Thanks to her gregarious nature, she has people she calls friends all over town. Her petite frame next to my taller, larger-boned body makes us look like mother and daughter, but between the two of us, she's much stronger, and she's quick to volunteer for tasks that let her prove it. At the end of a long day, when I let out a big sigh and say, "Whew, I'm really tired," she seems genuinely mystified as she asks, "Why always you so tired, Hiro?"

When I first arrived in Vietnam, I had expected the young women to be shy and wary of strangers, so Yun immediately stood out as someone special. Not only does she love to talk, but she has a way with words that can charm anyone. She engages complete strangers in conversation without the slightest reserve, and then often winds up getting into long discussions with them. She's well aware of the effect she has on people, too: whenever a problem presents itself, she simply says, "No worries. I am good talker." Then she puts her superb negotiating skills to work.

Without my ever asking, Yun basically took me under her wing as soon as I arrived in this country. She's been busily looking out for me ever since.

After asking Hai for a *sarsi* soda—a soft drink that tastes like medicine to me—Yun fishes a Japanese language text and a notebook from her bag.

"Teach this to me, please, Hiro," she says, opening her notebook.

The page she turns to contains a chaotic jumble of Vietnamese script mixed with Japanese hiragana, katakana, and kanji characters in all different sizes. Everything looks as though it's been scrawled in a great hurry, and I have trouble making anything out from a quick glance.

Yun attends classes at a Japanese language school three nights a week. At her request, I speak with her mostly in Japanese.

"*Shacho . . . wa . . . mo . . . kaeraremashita. Yomaremashita. Ikaremashita.* (The president already has gone home. Has read it. Has left.) This *-aremashita* form, for politeness, is same as passive form, yes?"

"That's right."

"But also have different one for politeness, yes?" she says, and reads from her notebook. "*Shacho . . . wa . . . mo . . . okaeri ni narimashita* (The president already has gone home) . . . ?" She says it as a question, as if asking for help.

"That's right. The basic form is *o*-blank *ni narimasu.*

The stem of the verb goes in the blank between *o* and *ni narimasu*, so for *kaerimasu* (go home), it's *o* plus *kaeri* plus *ni narimasu*. And that means for the past form it's *o* plus *kaeri* plus *ni narimashita*."

"Oh, yes. I now remember," she says confidently.

"Okay, then what do you get for *kikimasu* (hear)?"

Her self-satisfied expression instantly gives way to a nervous one. "*O . . . um . . . kiki . . . ni narimasu*."

I nod my approval, and she smiles happily as she looks at her notebook again.

"Next, um . . . um . . . *irasaimasu?*"

"*Irasshaimasu*. Doubled consonants have to be pronounced with a tiny break between them."

"*Ira . . . saimasu*."

"No, that's too much."

"*Irassaimasu*."

"That's better, but the sound after the break isn't *sa*. It's *sha. Irasshaimasu*."

She wrinkles her brow in concentration. "Um . . . *irasshaimasu*."

"That's right. Good. Repeat it five times."

"*Irasshaimasu, irasshaimasu, irasshaimasu, irasshaimasu, irasshaimasu!* It's good? *Irasshaimasu*." She glances at her notebook again. "This is polite word for three meanings, yes?"

"That's right. *Irasshaimasu* is a polite word that can mean 'go' or 'come' or 'is here.'"

"Go or come or is here. I learn. No problem." She opens her notebook again and double-checks her notes, then giggles once more. "I am very good at Japanese, yes?"

"I'd say you're so-so," I tell her.

"So-so? What it mean?"

"Not good and not bad."

"You are too hard, Hiro. Okay, next I have composition."

"You wrote it already?"

"Yes, I wrote it yesterday. Check it, please."

Yun pulls a folded sheaf of composition paper from her bag and spreads the sheets in front of me. I begin to read.

For a time I am absorbed in the world of her composition, but then Yun becomes bored waiting for me to finish and interrupts me.

"You like me, Hiro?"

"Yes, yes. I like you. I like you very much," I say, but recently she's been asking me this on a daily basis, so it's hard for me to muster much feeling.

She glares at me. "Say truly!" she scolds. "Say seriously!"

I've explained to her over and over that it's not customary in Japan to verbally reconfirm your affections all the time, but I haven't been able to get it to sink in.

"Oh come on!" I say in exasperation. "I told you yesterday that I like you—and the day before, and the day before that, and the day before that, too!"

Sometimes I feel as though the more I say I like her, the less I end up liking her; other times I feel as though saying it aloud every day actually makes it more real.

"How much?"

"As much as the sun."

I've given a variety of different answers to this question: as much as the whole world; as much as Japan; as much as the Pacific Ocean; as much as a ten-yen coin (I was in a bad mood).

"The sun! The sun! It's very big, yes?"

She beams. Day after day she asks me the same thing, and day after day she reacts with the same delight. I wish I could see a blueprint to the heart that responds with such undiminishing pleasure.

But as a matter of fact, Yun is perfectly well aware. She's perfectly well aware that the connection she and I share is not made up merely of the words we exchange. Between us exists a world in which neither Japanese nor English nor Vietnamese intervenes. It is a world that is unequivocally real—yet at the same time, seems impossible to believe.

TO PROTECT MYSELF FROM GETTING SUNBURNED, I pull on a hat and long nylon gloves that come up past my elbows. Next I lower goggles over my eyes to keep out the dust, then cover my mouth and nose with a cotton face mask to filter out exhaust fumes, before finally kicking my motorbike to life. Except it doesn't start on the first kick. My Honda Super Cub is a thirty-year-old granddaddy, and it can be a bit slow to get going. It belonged to one of Yun's neighbors, and she negotiated the purchase for me at a price I couldn't normally have gotten as a for-

eigner. She assured me it was in decent running condi-
tion, but the instruments and turn signals haven't worked
since I bought it. Nobody here seems to care about extra
features like that when they buy used bikes; the selling
price is determined solely by how well the engine runs.

The temperature feels like it must be a degree or two
above 30 Celsius. The breeze occasionally brings a breath
of coolness left over from the night air, but the heat of the
sun is already coming on strong. As always, the main road
is clogged with hundreds of motorbikes, merrily spewing
foulness into the air.

Morning starts early in Vietnam. At the university, the
first classes of the day begin around seven. I've heard,
though, that only a few students actually show up on
time. And I understand the same goes for the instructors.

At the Japanese Language Training Center where I
work, we have an early-morning staff meeting every
Monday. As a general rule, those who show up on time
for this meeting are also in the minority. It doesn't help
that the boss himself always comes late. I've learned to
shrug off this looseness about time: it's something I just
have to accept as part of working for a locally owned and
operated company. The lead Japanese instructor, Yamada,
who's been here three times as long as I have, has em-
braced it wholeheartedly and arrives dependably late.

The boss usually comes in around ten minutes after
we're due to start, and at that point the meeting com-
mences whether everyone else has arrived or not. Each
staff member reports on the previous week's classes and

his or her schedule for the week ahead. We discuss any problems we've encountered and ways we might improve our teaching. The boss's expectations are high, and if you don't produce the desired results, he can get pretty frosty or, worst-case scenario, you get axed. But as a native Japanese instructor, I feel quite safe. There are never as many of us as the center really needs, and not too surprisingly, we're more popular with the students, so something pretty drastic would have to happen before any of us would be shown the door. When it comes to teaching language, you really can't knock native speakers.

As in Japan, English is by far the most popular foreign language for people to study in Vietnam, so native English speakers are in especially high demand. But with so many companies from Japan setting up shop in recent years, Japanese has been rapidly on the rise. Since unemployment is high and foreign companies have a reputation for paying better wages, language schools are thriving.

English is supposed to be relatively easy for the population here because it's similar to their own language both in grammar and in the writing system. But many students have trouble freeing their pronunciation from the habits of their native tongue. In Vietnamese, the final p and t and x are usually silent; when they treat English words the same way, it makes them hard to understand.

By comparison, Japanese seems to give them quite a bit more difficulty as they try to learn it. For just one language, students have to learn three new sets of characters—the phonetic hiragana and katakana sets and the ideographic

kanji characters borrowed from Chinese. Vietnamese students of Chinese descent are already familiar with kanji,
so they usually learn the Japanese usage fairly quickly. But
many others find the Japanese writing system an almost
insurmountable barrier, with kanji as the biggest stum-
bling block. Yun is definitely among them, and I often see
her practicing several kanji over and over in her notebook
when she has a few free minutes. Besides the kanji barrier,
words written in katakana represent a major hurdle as
well. Once you've put in a reasonable amount of time on
kanji, you start to get a sense of certain rules that can give
you a pretty good guess about the meaning of words you
haven't seen before. But those rules are useless with
words written in katakana, most of which have been
adopted from completely different languages.

If I weren't already a native speaker of Japanese, I don't
think I'd want to learn it as a second language. It just
seems so inefficient and uneconomical compared to other
languages. There's no getting around the cumbersome
writing system—nor the inherent ambiguity of the language itself. I wonder how many of those who grow up
with the language have ever stopped to think how convo-
luted our jumble of three character sets is—with the
Roman alphabet often added to the mix as well.

The Japanese Language Training Center caters mainly
to employees of Japanese companies operating in Vietnam and trainees preparing for jobs in Japan. Our Vietnamese colleagues on the instructional staff can of course
speak Japanese, but many of them have surprisingly lim-

ited mastery for being teachers of the language. The center has about thirty full-time and part-time instructors altogether.

Our Vietnamese boss has a Ph.D. from the graduate division of the most competitive university in Japan, and he also lived there for a good many years, so he speaks fearsomely fluent Japanese. He has a hand in quite a few businesses here in Vietnam and maintains a wide network of contacts back in Japan as well. Whatever he says, goes: if something is white but he says it's black, then it's black, end of story. Any attempt to contradict him makes him angry, so my Vietnamese colleagues walk on pins and needles around him. While I can't endorse a managerial style that rewards only sycophants, I do respect the man's business savvy.

Once the reports are finished, the boss issues his instructions to us one by one.

"I see Yamada-sensei hasn't made it yet. She never does get here on time, does she?" He smiles. "Well, I won't dwell on that. Let's see, then, starting with Ito-sensei. You mentioned that two of the students in your IT group did poorly on the test. If they really don't have what it takes, then I should think the company will withdraw them from the class and that will be that. But if it's a reflection of your teaching, then we could have a major problem. Since you're Japanese and not so fluent in our language, the students may be testing you to see what they can get away with. I want you to put your foot down more, be a little stricter with them."

"Y-yes, sir."

"One way or the other, those students have to pass the Japanese Language Proficiency Test, so if you think they're not getting the class time they need, I can negotiate with the company to increase their hours. But if at all possible, I'd prefer to work within the current schedule. What do you think? Can you do it?"

"Yes, sir, I'll do my best," Ito says apologetically, as he nervously pushes up his glasses. He's thirty-three and he arrived in Vietnam just three months ago. He gave up a good, steady company job back in Japan for reasons only he can know, to work for low wages as an expatriate in far-off Vietnam. He's modest and shy, so he makes an easy target for the boss, and the students think they can take advantage of him, too.

"Now, Azuma-sensei."

Here we come. It's my turn.

"The classes at BMC are supposed to end this month, but I note that you've fallen a bit behind schedule. Of course, in this case, it's the company that asked to cancel classes a number of times for internal reasons, so you're not responsible for the lag, but they've asked us to increase class hours for the rest of the month, starting this week. Let's see, now. You have them on Tuesday and Thursday evenings, so starting tomorrow the classes will run from six to nine . . ."

Yikes! That's twice the hours!

". . . and they've agreed to put in a full day on Saturday,

so I want you to take them in the morning. Then Phuc-sensei can crack the whip in the afternoon."

Ouch. That's just cruel.

"To make sure valuable class time doesn't get wasted, you'll need to prepare detailed lesson plans ahead of time with plenty of solid drills. I want you and Phuc-sensei to put your heads together and work out a new schedule for the month with all the necessary changes and adjust-ments before the day is out."

"Yes, sir."

"So next we have Mikami-sensei. . . ."

THE FULL MEETING IS FOLLOWED BY A SMALLER GATH-ering of just the native Japanese staff. Even though she's our coordinator, Yamada still hasn't arrived. Hayashi, one of our part-timers, shows the rest of us some new exer-cise books that have just arrived from Japan. He may teach relatively few hours at the center, but he's in his early sixties and taught Japanese in several other countries before coming to Vietnam, so he's tremendously knowl-edgeable and is the best person to go to when you need advice. He's often hard to find, though, because he has a busy schedule teaching classes at universities and other Japanese language schools, and he comes to the center only on Mondays and Wednesdays.

Eight native Japanese instructors work here—three men and five women. Perhaps it goes without saying, but we're all certified to teach Japanese, either from majoring in college or through specialized training courses.

The meeting comes to an end. Ito takes a pill to settle his stomach before heading off to his class at a client's office. I watch his tall, slender figure from behind as he trudges out the door. Hayashi is summoned by the boss and gets up to go into the adjoining office. I have no classes until after noon, so I remain at my desk to work on lesson plans and the new schedule for BMC.

"Azuma-sensei, I'm busy today, so please go ahead and set up the schedule as you see fit. I'll leave it to you," Phuc calls from across the room, as she flees out the door.

Well, if she's going to be that way, maybe I'll just have to give her the tough stuff, I think, a little maliciously, when Yamada hurries in moments before her class is set to begin.

"What happened to you this morning?" I ask her.

"It's a long story. That jerk! Sometimes he just makes me so sick. It's his fault I'm late. Every time!"

The jerk she's referring to is her Vietnamese husband.

"You'll have to tell me all about it later," I say. "Right now you need to get to class."

"Well, then. Time to go let off some steam!" She windmills her right arm around as she heads to her classroom with a light step.

Yamada is thirty. She's the child of a mixed marriage between a Japanese father and a Vietnamese mother. She was born in Japan and grew up there, but six years ago she decided to move to Vietnam. Her parents still live in Japan.

Completely fluent in both languages, she's been teaching Japanese ever since she first arrived. Her strict methods intimidate students and teachers alike. I've had a number of opportunities to observe her classes, and I felt sorry for the students when I saw how they cowered in their seats—especially when they messed up and got one of her explosive reprimands in return. But she's not just putting on an act—she has the authority and knowledge to back up everything she says. I've learned a lot from her.

She's also the boss's favorite, and he's put her in charge of coordinating the Japanese staff, but she's always late for meetings. I've sometimes wondered if this split between strictness and looseness in her personality comes from being half Japanese and half Vietnamese.

AT NOON, YAMADA AND I WALK TO A NEIGHBORHOOD restaurant that's three minutes away. It's one of those places that doesn't look like much from the outside, and could be cleaner, but serves excellent food. She starts to tell me about her husband as we eat. We're surrounded by men whose open-collar white shirts, black or navy slacks, and synthetic-leather sandals—a sight one encounters at least once every three seconds in this city—mark them as office workers from nearby businesses. I always choose the stuffed bitter melon when I come here; she gets the stir-fried pork and bamboo shoots. The lunch options are arranged on large platters by the entrance; the waiter puts your selection onto a plate along with some rice.

"So you don't have to go home for lunch today?"

"I am so pissed at him! He was out all night! He didn't get home until this morning!"

Her loud voice, in a foreign tongue, causes people to turn and stare. We ignore them.

"Same story as before? Gambling?"

"No, just drinking. Though he could've been gambling while he drank, I suppose. That jerk—he finally came sauntering home late this morning. I can't leave the house if he's not home, because there's no one else to look after my boy."

Since her husband has no job, he handles child care and household duties while she's away at work. The boy is two, and his father is only twenty, so there's no denying the impression that a child has begotten a child. Yamada often says she feels as though she has two little boys to take care of.

"When I go home tonight, let me tell you, I'm gonna teach him a lesson."

A lesson? Just what kind of lesson, I wonder—but I'm too afraid to ask.

"I don't like his so-called friends. They're no good. They come looking for him, and he just takes off."

"The gambling part is scary. He's so young—aren't you worried someone might take advantage of him?"

"Oh, they already have. Didn't I tell you? Eight hundred dollars. Out the window in a single night."

"Eight hundred? In one night?"

As a point of reference, Yun's entire monthly income is equivalent to a little over a hundred dollars, which is about average here in Ho Chi Minh City.

"So, what did you do?"

"He said the interest would pile up and make things worse, and then we'd have the mafia knocking on our door, so what else could I do? I paid. Right away. The very same day."

"Yikes. But if you pay up that easily, won't they just try to sucker him again?"

"Yeah, I don't doubt they're trying. That's why I told him I'd divorce him if he ever let it happen again."

"His problem is that he's too gullible."

"They think he's an easy mark because he's from the country."

"Since you know they're up to no good, you should make him stop seeing them. What if they get him into amphetamines or something?"

"Oh, please. Stop trying to scare me. . . . Though I do have to admit it's possible, I suppose. That does it. He's really gonna get it good tonight."

Get what, exactly? The question is on the tip of my tongue, but again I can't bring myself to ask.

"Oh, are you free on Sunday? Can you come over? I'm cooking Japanese food. I'm asking the other teachers, too."

"Is the boss coming?"

"Are you kidding? If I invited him, nobody else would show."

"In that case, I'll come. I'll help cook."

"That's okay. I won't need any help. I'm just doing easy stuff."

"What're you making?"

"Somen noodles and Japanese-style curry rice."

"A starch and a starch?"

"I suppose I could put them together and make curried somen."

"That's not what I meant."

"No? You don't like somen and curry?"

"Sure I like them, and I haven't had either of them lately, so my mouth's watering already. Absolutely."

"So it's good then. It's decided."

"I'll bring some beer and wine."

"Oh, so you want to drink? You wanna get drunk?"

The hard-drinking Yamada lets out a gleeful little cackle.

BACK AT THE OFFICE, OUR TWO YOUNGEST JAPANESE colleagues, Kishimoto and Murai, are chattering back and forth as they work at their desks. The women are both in their early twenties and cute—a combination that makes them tremendously popular with their male students. From the day they first arrived, they've been acting like they're on an extended vacation, and it took them no time at all to find Vietnamese boyfriends. Since teaching is considered a sacred profession here, though, romances between female teachers and male students are highly frowned upon. And to make matters worse, someone reported seeing Murai engaged in indecent acts with her boyfriend in a nearby park, which caused a great deal of consternation. But even after being reprimanded by the boss, she seems completely remorseless: she apparently continues to spend time with her guy every day.

Though many of the instructors go home for the midday break, those who live too far away often use the nap room after lunch. When I first arrived, I was utterly flabbergasted to learn that my employer actually provided a place for taking afternoon naps, but I've gotten so I use the room myself from time to time.

At this hour of the day, the entire city grows quiet. Department store clerks put their heads down on the counter for a snooze, the ladies at the market fall sound asleep on their couches, and no one will pay you any attention if you show up to shop. At least that's the longstanding tradition. An increasing number of people seem to be giving up their siestas these days—especially those who work for the growing influx of overseas companies.

Yamada goes off to the nap room. I sit listening to the two young women blabbing on about their love lives as I try to do some more lesson prep. Before long, Ito returns. Soaked in sweat, he mops at his neck and brow with an old hand towel.

"You're really dripping," I say.

"No kidding."

He chugs hard on a bottle of mineral water. I watch his Adam's apple bouncing sharply up and down.

"Don't you think it's about time you got yourself a motorcycle? With all the different places you have to run around to, it might make life easier."

"No, no, that's not for me. I couldn't handle it. A bicycle's more my speed. There's no way I could drive a motorbike in all that chaos."

"That's what I thought, too, at first, but it just takes a little getting used to. It may look like total anarchy, but there's actually all these unspoken rules that everybody follows. Once you learn those rules, everything becomes automatic."

"But I've never ridden a motorcycle before, even in Japan."

"I never had either. That's nothing to worry about. It's easy. Just pretend you're on a bike in a video game."

"A bike in a video game?"

"Uh-huh. A car comes at you head-on in your own lane, an old lady totters out into the road, then a bike in the other lane loses control doing a U-turn and comes flying at you, or someone tries a risky pass in heavy traffic and nearly wipes you out, you know, and you have to somehow dodge all that stuff and make it to the finish line."

"You're too fearless, Azuma-sensei."

"Otherwise you're going to waste away, you know. You look like you've already lost weight in the last three months."

He was on the thin side to begin with, and he's been getting even thinner. Is he going to become so skinny he winds up indistinguishable from the locals?

"I know, I've dropped three kilos. If I keep this up, I'll be nothing but skin and bones in a year," he says, smiling faintly.

"Are you eating properly?"

"I haven't had much of an appetite. Vietnamese food doesn't seem to agree with me lately."

"When it's hot like this, you have to eat, or you'll collapse. Oh, here, have a guava," I say, picking up one of several lying on my desk and thrusting it at his chest, as if to force it on him.

"Thank you. I know that, but . . . I think maybe I'm just not made for this climate."

"You don't like the heat?"

"It's not that I don't like it, but when it's so relentlessly hot day after day like this, it seems to do something to my system."

"Your body just hasn't adjusted yet. I had the same problem my first three months or so. Sweating buckets. But once my body got used to it, I stopped sweating so much, and now the heat doesn't really bother me anymore."

"You really think I'll adjust?" he says dubiously.

"Oh, by the way, did you hear about the somen-and-curry party at Yamada-sensei's?"

"So it's somen and curry now? With me she was talking about doing *chirashi* sushi."

"Oh? Did she change her mind? Well, whatever she decides to have is fine with me. Are you going?"

"Yes, I'm looking forward to it."

"Good, then we can talk more on Sunday. Oh, if you intended to take a shower, the nappers will be getting up pretty soon, so you'd better hurry, or they'll all be taken."

"You're right," he says, and hurries out the door.

Ito's older than me, but he never really gives that impression when I'm talking to him.

MONDAY IS THE ONLY DAY OF THE WEEK WHEN everybody gathers together in one place at the same time. Since most of our classes are conducted at client sites, we're not required to check in at the center on days when we're only scheduled for other locations. As a result, some of us never see each other except on this first day of the work week.

The center's offices are on the second floor of a three-story building, where we also have four classrooms for our in-house program. The classes held here are mostly filled with trainees preparing to go to jobs in Japan. Below us on the first floor is another, somewhat mysterious business owned by the boss; the third floor houses the nap room, showers, and several conference rooms.

My current schedule has me teaching trainees here at the center every weekday afternoon, with client-site classes every morning except Monday, as well as three evenings a week. Once, when our native instructor count

was down, I had to work all day, every day, with classes
scheduled for the early morning, late morning, afternoon,
and evening. I argued that the quality of my classes was
suffering and I needed to reduce my load, but the boss apparently didn't agree and just kept drumming up new
clients. He's a businessman through and through—not an
educator.

I ENTER THE CLASSROOM AS THE BELL RINGS. THE
students are waiting politely in their seats. The students in
this class are all trainees scheduled to go to Japan after
completing a three-month-long language course here.
This particular group started a month ago. All fifteen of
the students are male.

They may be called trainees, but what they really are is
low-cost unskilled labor for Japanese companies. These
trainees have a high separation rate in Japan. I think probably there's some kind of powerful underground network
of Vietnamese nationals that they link up with once they
arrive. In fact, I imagine several of the men in this room
have been planning to desert from the start. But of
course, if their intentions were to become known beforehand, they'd never get to go to Japan, so they act like serious students. They're on their best behavior, knowing
that a bad attitude or lousy grades could ruin their chance
to go.

The citizens of Vietnam are not permitted to travel
freely outside the country the way we Japanese can. Even

just to get a tourist visa, they have to jump through a
bunch of hoops, such as providing a reliable guarantor in
Japan, and filing a detailed itinerary in advance.

To go to Japan as a trainee, you're required to pay a
kind of security deposit up front. At around ten thousand
U.S. dollars, the required sum is an astronomical figure
when you consider the local cost of living. So those who
set their sights on going scrape the money together by
turning to their relatives for help or taking out loans. If
they complete their contract term, they apparently get
the money back, minus various expenses and fees, but neither the boss nor I have ever been able to find out how
much that actually amounts to, or what exactly the various expenses and fees include.

The trainees' objective is all too clear: money, plain and
simple. The idea is to put away as much cash as they possibly can while they're overseas in order to buy themselves a house or start up a business when they return
home. If, after they get to Japan, they run away from the
company where they've been placed, they become illegal
residents and they lose their deposit money. But even
then, it's apparently more lucrative for them to strike out
on their own. The appallingly low wages paid to the
trainees represent a wholesale disregard for basic human
rights. Since they aren't Japanese citizens, their rights get
no respect. They work long hours every day from morning to night for some unbelievably paltry wage like sixty
thousand yen a month. Some companies put them under

tight restrictions, too, such as banning cell phones or re-
quiring in-house staff to be present anytime the trainees
meet Japanese people from outside the company.

Meanwhile, the placement agencies in Vietnam are
raking it in. And I figure the people who originally set up
the system are probably getting some pretty sweet returns, too.

The boss is not a broker himself—he's simply in the
business of providing Japanese classes for them—but his
true opinion of the whole trainee program is that it's an
outrage. When they get to Japan, the less-fortunate ones
wind up having to suffer through three long years of low
pay and atrocious working conditions, plus put up with
the racial biases that so many Japanese people have. But
the students come to the center with no idea of any of
that; they're just thrilled at the chance to go to a wealthy
country like Japan. Our job is solely to make sure they get
the language skills they will need while there.

This particular class ranges in age from eighteen to
thirty-five, and all but two of the fifteen are from small
villages. They'd never even been to the city before they arrived for their predeparture training. Some did not go to
high school and are unaccustomed to studying—in fact,
they don't have the slightest idea how to go about it. The
weakest of the students are hopelessly weak.

As soon as I enter the room, they rise to their feet without being prompted and perform their standard greeting
in unison.

"*Sensei, konnichi wa!* (Hello, teacher!)"

"*Konnichi wa! Minasan, genki desu ka?* (Hello! Are you all well?)"

"*Hai, genki desu. Sensei mo genki desu ka?* (Yes, we are well. Are you well, too, teacher?)"

"Yes, I'm fine."

"Sensei, take this, please."

A student named Nhan holds out a plastic bag containing something heavy.

"What is it?"

"Milk fruit."

"Wow. Thank you!"

"Milk fruit is very delicious."

The students exchange amused looks and whispers—no doubt because the Vietnamese name for this fruit means "breast milk."

"Sensei, we all go Dam Sen Park on Sunday," Nhan says with a smile. "Won't you go with us?"

"I'm sorry, but I have other plans this Sunday."

"Oh, I see. It's too bad. Do you have boyfriend, Sensei?" he leers. What a jerk.

"No."

"Oh, it's too bad!"

"I want Japanese girlfriend."

"I want to marry Japanese woman."

"Okay. In that case, you will have to study Japanese very hard, won't you?"

"Ye-e-es."

"Sensei, when will you go Japan?"

"That's a good question. I don't know."

"We will see you in Japan?"

"Sensei, I want to visit your house in Japan."

You want to visit that cramped two-room apartment, in that worn-out old housing block? That dismal place with all the warmth of a freezer, presided over by my spiritually bankrupt mother?

"If I'm home when you are in Japan, that would be great," I say. "All right then. Let's review what we learned yesterday. Long-san. *Senshu wa isogashikatta desu ka?* (Were you busy last week?)"

"*Hai, isogashikatta desu.* (Yes, I was busy.)"

"Quyet-san. *Kinou wa atsukatta desu ka?* (Was it hot yesterday?)"

"*Hai, achukatta desu.* (Yes, it was hotch.)"

"Hue-san. *Betonamu wa Nihon yori atsui desu ka?* (Is Vietnam hotter than Japan?)"

"*Hai, achui desu.* (Yes, it is hotcher.)"

"Everybody, repeat. *Atsui* (hot)."

"*Achui!*"

"*Atsui.*"

"*Achui!*"

"*Tsu!*"

"*Chu!*"

"Not *chu*. It has to be *tsu*. Repeat. *Tsu*."

We have already practiced the pronunciation of *tsu* at least a hundred times, but most of the students still lapse into *chu* if they're not being careful. The only difference between the two sounds is the position of the tongue against the top of the mouth. I sketch out a crude representation of the oral cavity on the white board, showing the tongue's more forward position for *tsu* in red and its position farther back for *chu* in blue. Then I point back and forth between the two colors as I pronounce *tsu, chu, tsu, chu* to make sure they hear the difference, and after that have them repeat the sounds with me over and over. When I open my mouth wide to show the students the position of my tongue as I say *tsu,* they all laugh.

Tsu is a difficult sound. There was a male vocalist from Hong Kong who was popular on Japanese TV a while ago, and he couldn't pronounce it properly either. I remember hearing him say *achui* for *atsui* and *ochukaresama* for *otsukaresama* ("thanks for your hard work"). I always wondered why nobody corrected him, but I suppose that kind of imperfection in his Japanese was actually part of his appeal.

"All right. That's enough practice for today on *tsu.* Now, let's see. Okay, Hien-san. Which do you like better, coffee or tea?"

"I like coffee better."

"Is that so? I like coffee better, too. Now, Minh-san. Which is faster to Hanoi, airplane or bus?

"B-b—"

"Bus?"

"B-b-b-bike . . ."

"Bike?"

"Bike . . ."

"Minh-san, nobody's going to Hanoi by bike. Your choice is airplane or bus. Which is faster, airplane or bus?"

"B-b-bus, bus."

"You're saying the bus is faster?"

"Yes, bus."

At this point, several others around him jump in to help, yelling out *"Hikooki!* (airplane)." In his characteristic manner, Minh scratches his head and looks up at me with bewilderment on his face.

"Minh-san, this is a *hikooki,*" I say, propping a picture of an airplane on the whiteboard. I add a picture of a bus. "And this is a *basu.* We studied these words yesterday and the day before, do you remember? What is this?" I ask him, pointing to the bus.

"B-b-basu."

"All right. Then, what is this?" I ask again, this time pointing to the picture of the airplane.

He looks blank.

"It's a *hikooki. Hikooki. Hikooki.* Say it for me."

"Hi-hi-hi-hikoki."

"No, *hikooki.* The *o* is long. *Hikooki."*

"Hi-hiko . . . hikooki."

"Yes, that's right. *Hikooki."*

"Hi-hikooki. Hikooki."

"The choices are *hikooki* and *basu.* Which is faster to Hanoi, *hikooki* or *basu?"*

"Hi-hikooki."

"Yes, very good," I say, and Minh scratches his head again with a relieved smile.

"Minh-san, I need you to study harder. Are you studying at home, too?"

"Y-y-yes. Yes."

"Sensei, Minh-san work hard every day. He study at
home."

It is Minh's roommate Long who speaks up in support
of his friend. Long obviously has an aptitude for languages.
He's the best student in the class. He also serves as the class
leader, coordinating various things among the students.

But after studying every day for a month, Minh has yet
to fully master his hiragana and katakana. Since that
means he can't read his textbook properly, he keeps falling
further and further behind the others. I suspect he has
trouble expressing himself in his native tongue as well.
When someone has a poor command even of his own
language, how can he expect to master an altogether different one? It makes me want to give up on him sometimes, but when I see how valiantly he tries, I feel like I
need to somehow find a way to pull him through.

The students in the class have an extremely strong
sense of solidarity. They stand up for each other and help
each other out. There are aspects of their world and
the rules they live by that they would never reveal to an
outsider—especially one who is their teacher, and a member of the opposite sex. As with us Japanese, they separate
what they really think or feel from the face they put on for
others—and they lie.

. . .

AFTER CLASS I SIT DOWN WITH MAI, ONE OF MY CO-teachers, to discuss how the group is progressing. Mai is four years younger than me, so she's sort of like a little sister, but she's also a highly devoted and demanding teacher and I know I can depend on her. She's good friends with Yun, too. The three of us often share meals or hang out at each other's homes.

The first time Mai invited me to her place, I was astonished at its tiny size. She rents a room in what is otherwise a regular single-family house, and she lives there with her two sisters in a space that's only about the size of a six-mat tatami room. They even cook their meals right there in the room, on a small gas burner.

Mai also invited me along once when she and her sisters went home to visit their parents in Vung Tau for several nights. Her family are adherents of Caodaism, so I was greeted by the Cao Dai religion's Divine Eye when I arrived. This is a twentieth-century religion founded in Vietnam, based on principles drawn from Buddhism, Confucianism, Taoism, Christianity, and Islam—mixing them together in a kind of religious stew. An eye inside a triangle, called the Divine Eye, is its main symbol. At around four o'clock each morning, the sound of Mai's grandmother chanting scripture began echoing through the single-level, two-bedroom house. Grandma's room was also the altar room, Mom and Dad had their own room, and the rest of us slept on the floor of the sitting room. Mom got up even earlier than Grandma to go to her job at the market. Dad rose before dawn as well, to water the flowers and shrubs in the garden. We city dwellers in the sitting room were the only ones who waited until daylight to rouse ourselves.

Mai and I are still talking about the class when Nam comes by. Looking up, Mai asks him something too fast for me to follow, and gets a happy nod in return. Nam is the coordinator of the Vietnamese instructional staff. One of his trademark gestures is the way he holds out his pinkie when he writes with chalk. With his light complexion and effeminate manner—not to mention the way he squeals and shrieks at soccer games—most people would probably assume that he's gay, but he's not. Although he's obviously bright, he's not very well organized, so the boss gets annoyed with him a lot. When he speaks with Japanese people, he responds to practically everything by saying daijobu ("no problem"), even when things are not daijobu at all—which strikes me as typically Vietnamese of him.

Nam shouts something toward several of the Vietnamese staff who are sitting in a circle across the room, eating fruit.

They all let out a cheer. "All right!"

"What?" I ask Mai. I hadn't been able to catch what Nam said. "What happened?"

"Our Teachers' Day bonuses will be up from last year."

"Excellent! That's great news!"

"Yes, it makes everybody happy!"

November 20 is Teachers' Day in Vietnam. On this day, teachers receive all sorts of gifts from their students.

Some are elaborate handcrafted items that leave you deeply moved by the tremendous amount of time and effort that you know went into them. I still have a hand-decorated garland and a jar filled with dozens of tiny paper cranes that I got last year. The instructors from Japan are especially popular on this day.

But I suppose it's pretty much only during the first year that you truly appreciate all the special attention you get. After a certain point, you grow tired of the constant inquisitiveness, the curious looks, the endless invitations, and the virtually identical repetition, ad nauseam, of the same conversations. Gradually you start to pull away from the students. It's not that you dislike them. You've simply grown tired, both in body and in spirit. You know the students' intentions are harmless, and they are simply being their sincere but naïve selves, but that only serves to deepen the sense of fatigue that you feel.

In Vietnamese society, there are many things that you have to be a native to understand. A great deal goes on that someone looking in from the outside simply cannot grasp. Rules and norms exist that everybody automatically knows, without anything ever needing to be said. I think they are a great deal like us Japanese in this way. I don't doubt that anybody looking in from the outside has a hard time comprehending us, too. We have often been called inscrutable. We, too, have a great many unspoken understandings that we share. Living as an outsider in such countries is extremely exhausting.

CHAPTER TWO

I GET HOME FROM WORK AND TAKE A quick shower before coming back down to Hai's café to wait for Yun. I sit side by side with Hai at a table on the outer fringes of the yellow light that radiates from the bulbs inside the store. We watch a little boy ride his tricycle back and forth on the quiet street in front of us as we snack on some acerolas I bought on my way home. At the table next to us, three middle-aged men I recognize as residents of the building above the café are carrying on a heated card game. There's money at stake and high-pitched whoops and shouts erupt as they play.

Vietnamese is a tonal language, much like Chinese—though the northern dialects have six tones, and the southern dialects five, compared to the Chinese four. The tones span a considerable range, with the rising tones reaching quite high. I suppose it's because of this that so many Vietnamese men seem to have such high voices. When I see some scruffy-looking men twice my age chattering away like a couple of birds tweeting and chirping at each other, it sometimes gives me a little shudder. Then on top of that, so many of them have these swishy mannerisms and walk about with their arms looped together or around each other's shoulders that you'd swear they must all be gay.

I find myself wondering why so many of the men in Southeast Asia seem like such wimps, while so many of the women come across as balls of fire. Is there some law of nature that turns men slothful and women industrious in places where it's hot all year long?

I ask Hai for another coffee.

"You sure do like coffee, don't you," she says, as if she doesn't entirely approve. She rises to her feet and goes to the stand where the coffee beans and such are kept, directly behind where I'm sitting.

"It's because Vietnamese coffee is so good," I say, twisting halfway around to look at her. "Especially yours."

The robust flavor and sweet, chocolaty notes of Vietnamese coffee is a perfect match for my taste. To a tall, slender glass filled with a mountain of crushed ice you add a small amount of hot black coffee so strong it actually appears to be thick, then churn it up and down with a long-handled spoon. The syrupy, hot liquid thins as it

chills, and turns into iced coffee of just the right strength.
The rattle and slosh of the ice as the spoon thrusts up and
down reveal how seasoned a coffee drinker you are.

"You foreign women are all so fond of coffee," Hai
says. "I can't stand the stuff myself."

She comes back with a glass of ice and a filter cone
filled with fresh-ground coffee and hot water, which she
places in front of me and sits down. It will take a minute
or two for the coffee to finish dripping.

"You don't drink coffee?"

"Never," she says, making a face as if the very idea is
preposterous.

When you go to cafés, you usually see Vietnamese
women drinking some kind of juice or soda instead of
coffee. The coffee drinkers in such places are all men. Yun
dislikes coffee, too, and never touches it. Like alcohol, it's
considered a man's drink, and there's the definite sense
that it's not proper for a woman to be seen gulping down
glass after glass in public. By the same token, cigarettes
are for men only, and women are not supposed to smoke.
On occasion you do run across some tough-looking old
lady at the market or a hooker trolling for customers at a
bar puffing away on a cigarette, but those are the excep-
tions, and a female office worker or teacher who smokes
would be regarded as a scandal.

It all seems rather stifling to me, but I don't want to
simply excuse myself as a foreigner and go around doing
whatever I please. On the other hand, I don't want to re-
strain my behavior so much that I build up stress, either.

So on issues like this that involve cultural differences, I've tried to gauge how far I can safely permit myself to go by asking Yun for her advice, as well as by paying close attention to how people are reacting around me.

"Do you plan to stay in Vietnam permanently?" Hai asks, changing the subject.

"It's hard to say."

"I think you should marry a Vietnamese and settle down here."

"Marry a Vietnamese? We-e-ell . . ."

"My customers here include many eligible young bachelors, so I will introduce you."

"When you say young, though, they're probably younger than I am, aren't they? You do realize I'm twenty-eight already. Twenty-nine by the Vietnamese count, actually."

"Oh, that's right. You're pretty old. Foreigners look younger to me, so I keep forgetting. But that's okay. You're a foreigner, so it doesn't matter if you're older."

In Vietnam, it's considered undesirable for the woman to be older.

"So do you know any good-looking guys who have lots of money?" I ask, playing along.

"Oh yes, oh yes."

"Somebody who speaks English or Japanese?" Living with someone who speaks only Vietnamese would be draining.

"Yes, at least somebody who speaks English. You should marry him. Right away."

"Yes, ma'am."

Except for a young fellow who comes to help out for a few hours here and there, Hai manages the shop all by herself. Until recently her sister Ba was always on duty as well. Like Hai, Ba was quite short, but in contrast to Hai's slender build, Ba was on the plump side. Having both lost their husbands in the war, the sisters were very close, but all of a sudden, last month, the shop remained shuttered for several days, and when it finally reopened, Ba was nowhere to be seen. I learned from one of the neighbors that she'd died after failing to move her bowels for three weeks.

Following her sister's death, Hai reopened the shop as if nothing had changed—except that during those lulls in business when she used to gab with her sister, she now stands forlornly by herself at the front of the store, in silence. It makes my heart ache.

In this country you meet a great many women like Hai and Ba—women in their middle years or older who lost their husbands during the war and have been left single again. When you look at the over-thirty population, women outnumber men by a significant ratio. And it's more difficult here than in Japan for a woman to go through life by herself. The custom is for children to look after their parents in their old age, and since being single means having no children, their twilight years are destined to be lonely ones. With the population of women being so much larger, it's a buyer's market for the men. The balance of the sexes is completely out of whack. I recall the war correspondent Koichi Kondo writing about this, too—which is to say, it was already this way thirty years ago, and the passage of time has yet to bring any significant change to the situation.

The *doi moi* reforms in the late 1980s sparked economic development, and today the generation of young people born after the war is on the rise. Blessed with the chance to go to school and acquire valuable skills, they're now in line for high-paying opportunities in the job market. Meanwhile, their older sisters who went through the war are left to eke out a meager existence running small cafés and such on the street. So here's Hai, providing service with a smile to the young kid who comes riding up on a big high-end Japanese motorcycle to ask for a pack of cigarettes while talking on an expensive late-model cell phone. On the rear seat of his bike sits a fair-skinned young woman in sunglasses, a halolike ring of light reflected from her long, shiny black hair.

Hai, for her part, owns neither a motorcycle nor a cell phone. Her skin is dark, while her short-cropped hair lacks any sheen and shows a good bit of gray. She never wears anything but the traditional, pajamalike *ao ba ba*. It leaves me wondering why it has to be this way. I know she's worked a whole lot harder in her life than any of these young upstarts.

But such is the way the world goes round.

I LET MY MIND WANDER UNTIL ALL OF A SUDDEN someone drops into the chair beside me with a heavy

thud. Turning, I see that it's Kanazawa, a fellow expatriate
who lives nearby.

"Did you just wake up?" I ask, looking at his tousled
hair.

"Uh-huh. I guess maybe three hours is a bit too long for
a nap." He yawns sleepily and rubs his eyes.

"You do realize it's evening already?"

Without even waiting for him to ask, Hai brings him a
glass of coffee and sets it down in front of him.

Kanazawa rents a room in an imposing four-story villa
three doors down the street from the café. The house is
approved for nonresidents, so the owner rents rooms to
foreigners and to overseas Vietnamese who are back in
the country for short stays. He actually lives in the United
States, and his younger sister manages the property.

Kanazawa is essentially an expatriate NEET—"not cur-
rently engaged in employment, education, or training"—
though, at age thirty-six, he technically falls outside the
range we normally associate with the term in Japan. Since
the day I first met him, he's been saying that he intends to
enroll in a Vietnamese language school, but he has yet to
do anything about it. Like so many of the local men, he
spends prodigious amounts of time idling away the hours
in cafés.

"I'm getting ready to go for some papaya salad with
Yun. Would you like to come along?" I suggest.

"I feel more like a buffet today, so I think I'll pass."

"Where are you thinking of going?"

"The Sofitel Plaza."

"What kind of food do they have?"

"Pan-European, I guess. French and Italian and such."

"I can't say that sounds particularly appetizing."

"Sure, fine. So stick with the local cuisine. It's cheaper. And probably healthier."

He starts jabbing his tall spoon up and down in his coffee. I listen quietly to the rattling ice.

The men at the next table erupt in a mixture of shouts. One of them has apparently won big. The Vietnamese love to gamble. From table games to soccer, they're always eager to put money on the outcome of some event.

"Hi-i-i! I come!" Yun calls out as she zooms up on her motorcycle and stops in front of the table where we're sitting.

"Good evening, Kanazawa-san!" she says.

"Hey there."

"You go to eat with us, Kanazawa-san?" she asks, her eyes moving back and forth between him and me.

"No. I have other plans today."

"Sometime soon, you go to eat with us, yes?"

I stand and straddle the rear seat behind Yun.

"Sure, sounds good," Kanazawa says, raising his right hand to wave as we drive off.

Yun steers her bike toward the papaya salad cart that sets up shop in front of Van Hoa Park along Hai Ba Trung Street.

"Kanazawa-san always surprise me. He do nothing. No work. No study."

"And he sleeps a lot," I say.

Yun has good instincts as a driver, but she also tends to be a bit reckless—going too fast, making sudden turns, passing when there isn't room—so I keep nagging her to drive more cautiously. But sometimes I'm convinced she's actually amusing herself by testing to see how much she can scare me. At times like that I make her switch places with me, and treat her to a taste of her own medicine, driving even more recklessly than she does. Since I had no previous experience on motorbikes back in Japan, I learned to drive from scratch under Yun's tutelage after arriving here. With less than two years' experience and still no license, my erratic driving can very quickly put alarm in her voice.

"Carefully, Hiro, carefully. More slowly. More slowly," I hear her repeating behind me, as if chanting a prayer.

IN FRONT OF THE ENTRANCE TO VAN HOA PARK IS an open area much like a parking lot that the enterprising operators of the papaya salad cart are using to conduct business—no doubt without any special authorization. Diners sit on the curb separating the sidewalk from the street, or on a similar curb around the base of the trees, or wherever else they can find a perch. Once you've chosen a spot, someone comes to take your order. The pushcart where the salads are actually fixed is parked on the opposite side of the street, and experienced waiters employed by the owners shuttle back and forth across the roadway balancing numerous plates in both hands as they deftly dodge the endless flow of motorcycle traffic. I wondered at first why they went to such trouble when it would be so much easier to simply set their cart up on the park side of the street, but to have the cart over here would apparently run up against some law or prohibition that makes it impossible to do business that way. The place is tremendously popular, with lots of loyal customers always crowded around. It's where I go, too, whenever I want papaya salad. After trying the salad served by other vendors a number of times, I know the version they serve here is by far the best. Papaya is supposed to be good for moving your bowels, so any time I think I'm getting constipated, I come by and treat myself to two or three platefuls. Yun and I both have a tendency to get stopped up.

"Yun, are you constipated again?" I ask her.

"Yes, constipated. One week."

"You haven't pooped in a whole week?"

"I think again I get hemorrhoids maybe."

"Uh-oh. More hemorrhoids could mean another operation. You better eat lots of salad."

"Yes, I try hard."

Seeing the earnest look in her eye, I burst out laughing.

"What?" she asks.

"I was just remembering your surgery," I explain, still smiling at the memory.

"Not nice to laugh." She frowns. "Hurt very bad."

"It was pretty scary, wasn't it? That hospital."

"Yes, very scary, and very painful."

. . .

YUN HAD TO HAVE A HEMORRHOIDECTOMY LAST
month. She was wailing in pain and turning red in the
face, so I finally took her to the doctor. The small hospital
she directed me to looked pretty old. It was dark and dank
inside, and didn't seem very clean. We arrived right at the
beginning of the afternoon clinic hours, but the doctor
wasn't back from lunch yet, so we had to wait for what
felt like forever. With no air-conditioning or fans in the
waiting room, it was so sweltering we had to mop our
sweat constantly with hand towels. As we waited, other
patients continued to arrive in a steady stream.

"Looks like a lot of people have hemorrhoids," I said.

"Yes, a lot of people have," Yun replied, a faint smile
tugging at her lips, even as her eyes brimmed with tears.
Since first arriving in the waiting room, she'd been going
back and forth between sitting, then standing, then sitting
again; even when she was sitting she would jiggle her
knee incessantly, unable to simply sit still. She has always
hated hospitals, and she'd gritted her teeth and tried to
avoid coming for as long as she possibly could before finally breaking down and letting me bring her in.

A middle-aged doctor with a sloppy, unbuttoned white
coat—he was a man of unusual girth for this country—
appeared from somewhere and swept into the examination room. Moments later, Yun's name was called.
Despite being so numb with fear that she hardly knew
what was what anymore, she appeared deceptively calm

as she rose from her chair. Feeling a little like a mother bringing her child to the doctor, I accompanied her as far as the doorway.

With the door apparently always left open, I was able to watch from there as the doctor initially questioned Yun about her symptoms. Before long he motioned her toward an examination table at the back of the room and drew a curtain around it for privacy. Through a slit in the curtain I caught glimpses of something silvery that looked like scissors in the doctor's hand.

Does she have the protruding kind? . . . Are those scissors properly sterilized? Isn't he going to give her an anesthetic? The questions swirling inside my head were suddenly interrupted by an ear-piercing *Aaagh!* that rang out through the entire waiting room. Even though I wasn't the one undergoing the surgery, an icy chill gripped my spine. For a moment, I thought I might throw up.

I don't believe it! He obviously didn't use anesthetic! He just took those scissors and snipped!

Feeling faint, I lowered myself onto the nearest sofa. My eyes met those of a woman about my own age sitting across the room. She offered me a nervous smile. I got the feeling she was fighting hard to keep her fears from getting the better of her. She was a lovely woman, but did she have hemorrhoids, too? Unable to muster up a smile, I grimaced as if to say, *That sounded painful.* Looking around the room, I could see anxiety on everyone's face.

Less than ten minutes after she'd cried out in pain, Yun came shuffling out of the examination room.

"You're all done?" I asked in surprise.

With a single small nod, she collapsed onto the sofa.

"You're not going to be admitted?" I went on, peering in at her tightly drawn face.

"Be . . . admitted?" she asked back, her voice so weak I could barely hear.

"You're not staying in the hospital overnight?"

"Not . . . staying," she managed to squeeze out. I could see the blood draining from her face.

The lady across the room who'd been watching Yun with great interest was next to be called. When she got to her feet, Yun raised her hand in a gesture of support. A look of resolution came into the woman's eyes as she nodded back and stepped into the examination room.

Yun lay with her head in my lap, limp from her ordeal, while I gently rubbed her shoulders and stroked her back, hoping to soften her pain at least a little. A constant refrain of low moans emerged from her throat. Then all of a sudden, without any warning, she rose to her feet and started unsteadily toward the door. Caught by surprise, I blankly watched her go for a moment before shaking myself awake and hurrying after her.

"Wait, Yun. Are you sure you're okay?"

She didn't answer. I was alarmed by the way she was sweating.

"I really think you should rest a little more before we go."

"No . . . problem. Get . . . motor . . . bike."

No problem? Who was she kidding? She looked ready
to keel over at any moment.

"I want you to rest a little more first," I said again.

"No problem!" She was determined to leave.

"Then let's take a taxi, okay?"

She'd flatly rejected my suggestion of a taxi on the way
here, but I thought it was worth a try.

"No! . . . Motorbike!"

Yun dislikes automobiles because she gets violently car-
sick. I've noticed that many Vietnamese seem susceptible
to motion sickness, perhaps because they're not so accustomed to riding in cars.

"All right. I'll go get the motorcycle, so you wait right
here by the door."

Realizing it was a waste of time to try to change her
mind, I hurried to the parking lot. When I returned to the
entrance, she was crouched over in pain. I helped her
onto the back of the bike and we set off.

"Slowly . . . gently . . . please," she said.

She was riding sideways and listing carefully in an effort to keep the surgical site from hitting the seat. *Ooof.*
Every so often she let out a groan and pressed her face
hard against my back. I kept my speed down and drove as
smoothly as I could, while also hurrying to get her home
as quickly as possible. We stopped en route to buy some
pain pills, and when we reached my apartment I made her
take some right away as I was getting her into bed. Bury-
ing her face in the pillow, she continued to moan in pain

for a time, but eventually the medicine began to do its job and she drifted off to sleep. She woke up once in the middle of the night and drank a glass of water, then slept like the dead until morning.

After remaining in bed the entire next day, she returned to her normal routine the day after that. A doughnut-shaped cushion became her best friend for a time, and since she couldn't drive her motorbike, I ferried her to and from work. She apparently still experiences occasional twinges of pain even today.

IT SADDENS ME A LITTLE TO THINK THAT MY MIND now invariably associates papaya salad with constipation, hemorrhoids, and that scary trip to the hospital. As we sit on a curb framing the base of a tree, munching on our salads, we are interrupted by a steady stream of visitors—a man who seems barely more than skin and bones hawking coconut water; a little girl wanting to sell us chewing gum; an old woman begging for money.

I'm feeling thirsty so I buy some coconut water. This clear liquid, found inside green coconuts, is sold everywhere around town, and not only is it cheaper and easier to buy than mineral water, but its relatively mild sweetness makes it the perfect thirst quencher. It's a curiously ambiguous drink. Some people claim it's good for your skin so you should have some every day, while others warn that drinking too much will make your periods stop.

When I ask for one, the man lops off the top of the hard coconut shell with a machete and inserts a straw before handing it to me.

"I haven't seen Dat today," I say.

"He soon come, I think."

Dat is a nine-year-old boy we've become friendly with. He sells chewing gum, but as a sales incentive, he also offers his paying customers a massage. A boy his age ought to be in school, but he isn't. His mother sells dried squid from a cart, and my guess is that he doesn't have a father. Yun has tried to help him out in various ways so that he can go to school, but all her efforts have been in vain. He apparently has no interest in classroom education.

The beggar woman is still standing there with her right hand extended. Yun gives her a little something and she finally moves on to the young couple sitting next to us.

"She have no family. It's why she ask for money. Old women have very hard time."

Yun is generous about handing out money or food to beggars of advanced age. With no children or anyone else to help them and no longer able to work, destitute seniors are forced to depend on the mercy of strangers in their final years.

There are legions of child beggars as well. Some are street children who have no parents, but others are in effect working for their parents. Even then, if it's because their families are so poor that they depend on the young ones' begging money to make ends meet, I can sympathize. Unfortunately, you also have cases where the parents are simply too lazy to work: they send their kids out to beg because they know people will feel sorry for them, and then live off what the little ones bring home. You see children with every stitch of clothing and every open patch of skin covered in dust and grime, but you also see children wearing school uniforms, looking clean and tidy.

Yun's family used to be poor, too, and she tells me that she sold chewing gum for a time when she was little.

Another common sight around town is people with disabilities of various kinds, such as blindness or an amputated leg. The first time I encountered a man crawling facedown next to the ground on a rolling plywood contraption slightly bigger than a skateboard, I couldn't quite believe my eyes. He was missing both his right arm and right leg altogether, while his left leg was twisted unnaturally up over his back, and he had to use his only remaining good limb to propel himself along the ground. Next to his head was an empty tin can for people to drop money into.

People who get around on something akin to an oversized skateboard—in some cases with a string attached for someone else to pull—are not a particularly rare sight. And in any case, the number of beggars is large, so if you tried to help them all you'd clean yourself out in no time. On the other hand, the population of wealthier people seems to be growing steadily, and the rich keep getting richer. Just like in Japan, where money flows, it flows with the force and din of Niagara Falls, and where it doesn't, it trickles almost imperceptibly, like a stream about to dry up.

"He come, he come," Yun says, pointing off to the left. I see Dat walking with his box of chewing gum in one hand. "Dat! Da-a-at!" she yells at the top of her lungs, waving a hand high over her head.

Dat sees us and breaks into a smile as he waves his skinny arm and starts our way. He's a good-looking boy, and I'm sure he'll turn into a handsome young man someday, but he's thin as a rail.

As soon as we exchange greetings, he begins rubbing my shoulders. He has remarkably strong hands, considering how bony he is. While he works on my muscles, squeezing and pounding, he strikes up a rapid-fire conversation with Yun. When he's done with my shoulders, he also massages the palms of my hands.

After finishing my massage, Dat sits down next to Yun and continues talking to her with a cheerful smile. Their voices recede into the background of my consciousness as I watch the endless stream of motorcycles flowing by in front of us. Perhaps because she has a naturally low voice, Yun's tones have a relatively narrow range, and it's hard for me to follow her Vietnamese.

Squeak. Squeak. I turn toward the mildly ear-grating sound and see a bicycle cart with dried squid hanging from it pedaling slowly our way. It is Dat's mother. He hops up as soon as he sees her.

"Bye," he says, and dashes off to join her.

I follow the two with my eyes as they move off into the

distance. In the deepening blue light after sundown, they slowly melt away into the scenery, until they are completely absorbed by it and disappear from sight.

There are so many different kinds of parent and child.

Parent and child. Parent and child. Parent and child.

I suppose I'm at an age when I really ought to become a parent, but I simply don't think I'm capable of raising a child yet. You just pick it up as you go, after you have the child, people tell me, but I remain utterly unable to imagine what it is I'm supposed to pick up, or how.

"Temperature is cooler now," Yun says, reaching both arms high over her head in a big stretch.

I feel at ease when I'm with Yun. That's why I'm always with her. As the time we've shared between just the two of us continues to grow, it sometimes feels as though that shared time is becoming so concentrated and thick that it might congeal and stop flowing, and that frightens me. She and I are a lot alike in certain ways. Perhaps this comes from similar experiences we had in our past.

When I squeeze Yun's sweet little hand, she smiles and squeezes firmly back.

IT WAS ON MY SECOND DAY IN VIETNAM THAT I FIRST met Yun.

As Yamada and I came out of the center to go to lunch, after she had given me my orientation that morning, I noticed someone draped across the top of a motorcycle

parked in the shade of a tree next to the gate. This was
Yun. When she saw us, she sat up and called out a greeting to Yamada. She had an orange cap on her head and
she was wearing faded jeans with a pastel blue T-shirt.
With her medium build, short haircut, and androgynous
features, I was momentarily unsure whether I was looking at a he or a she, but then I noticed the slight swells in
her shirt and knew she was a woman. Squinting beneath
the glare of the sun, she came over and began talking fa-
miliarly with Yamada in Vietnamese.

I studied her profile as they spoke. Her voice had a
certain huskiness that seemed the perfect match for her
boyish haircut and attire. Her dyed, light brown hair com-
plemented her deep brown eyes and lustrous, golden
brown skin, and the two tiny hoops of gold she had
placed in her earlobes blended so well with her complexion that they seemed almost to be a part of her. Beads of
sweat sparkled like gems on her brow and neck. I watched
as one of them trickled in a straight line down her temple
and plummeted to the parched ground at her feet.

I gazed at the fallen drop of sweat. A dark brown spot
spread into the pale brown earth and quickly began to
fade.

I felt a stirring of the ovenlike air around me and raised
my eyes. Her short hair glistened in the sunlight as it rip-
pled gently in the breeze.

"You are new teacher?" she asked in slightly stilted
Japanese, looking me directly in the eye from close range.

In the sparkle of her eyes, I sensed something akin to the sexually charged glances I'd received at times from men, and it startled me.

"Yes. My name is Azuma. Nice to meet you," I said, trying to sound unruffled. But a smile that seemed to say she could see right through me tugged at her lips as she responded:

"My name is Yun. I am, very pleased, to meet you."

I remained uncertain what to make of that unsettling glimmer in her eyes.

Since I said nothing further, she went back to chatting with Yamada in Vietnamese. I stood listening blankly to the sound of their voices.

A short while later, Mai emerged from the building and called out to Yun.

"*Sensei, sayonara,*" said Yun as she threw her legs astride the motorcycle and drove off with Mai riding behind her.

Several days later, Yun suggested that Yamada and I join her and Mai for dinner. It was too soon yet for me to have really gotten my bearings in Vietnam, so Yamada and Mai were full of advice on how to smooth my adjustment, while Yun seemed amused by the difficulties I was having.

After that, the outgoing Yun began inviting me to do things with her at every opportunity. Since I was new to the country and I neither knew my way around nor had other friends to casually go to lunch or dinner with, I was grateful for her thoughtfulness. It wasn't long before the two of us were eating dinner together more and more frequently. Yamada and Mai tended to eat at home with their families, but Yun wasn't so fond of home cooking and liked to go out. She knew the kinds of places only a native could know—the restaurants with the best food, the cafés with the best atmosphere—and she introduced me to them one by one. It made her happy to hear me cry out over how delicious the food was.

We could feel ourselves being drawn more strongly to each other every time we met.

This was the first time I'd ever felt so strongly attracted to a member of my own sex. I was beginning to develop feelings for Yun that I'd never experienced before.

Riding behind Yun on her motorcycle soon after we first met, I debated whether or not I should put my arms around her waist, but couldn't quite work up the nerve. When I continued to hesitate, she reached around to pull my hands forward one at a time and plant them on her stomach. So then I clasped my hands together at about the level of her belly button and awkwardly bowed my arms around her trying not to touch either her stomach or her back.

One day, when I was in the driver's seat, Yun wrapped her arms around me so tightly that I could feel her heart thumping against my back; her breath tickled my neck as she spoke practically right into my ear. All of a sudden I found myself getting turned on as I drove, almost to the point of crying out. I was flabbergasted. Nothing like that had ever happened to me before, and I had no idea what

to make of it. Yun touched me without the slightest hesitation, as if it was the most natural thing in the world for
her to do, but coming from a country where members of
the same sex rarely have any physical contact, I couldn't
help worrying what others might think, especially at first.
Before long, though, I concluded that I didn't need to be
concerned about such things here. I gradually grew accustomed to wrapping my arms more tightly around Yun
when I was on the back of her motorcycle.

Each evening when we said goodbye, I felt pangs of
loneliness and had a hard time pulling myself away, even
though I knew I'd see her the next day. Our routine was
for her to drop me off before heading home by herself
along the darkened streets; then she'd text my cell phone
when she was safely there. As I lay in bed drifting off to
sleep, I often found myself remembering Yun's talkative
eyes, or her delicate smell, or the moist, silky-smooth
sheen of her skin, or the tiny beads of sweat I'd seen
standing out on her neck.

"ARE YOU SEEING ANYONE, YUN?"

   "No, I not seeing anyone now."

   "But you were before?"

   "Yes, before."

   "What kind of person?"

   "He is older. President of small company. How about
you?"

   "Me? What?"

"Are you seeing anyone?

"No."

"But you were before, yes? What kind of person?"

I didn't answer. *She said "he."* The person was a he, I thought to myself. Which meant . . . what? My own relationships before this had all been with men. Had that been true for Yun, too? But if so, then what were those signals I kept getting from her? There was something suggestive in them, like I might expect from a man who saw me as an object of sexual desire, not from someone who's just a friend. We both seemed to be looking at each other as a person we might become more than just friends with, and I felt a strong sexual charge pass between us when we exchanged glances. Being in Yun's presence made me experience the same extreme self-consciousness I remembered from when I'd been smitten with a guy; the slightest little thing would set my heart beating furiously and make my face burn. But I also felt like she was looking out for me, so there was no need for protective fronts. I could be completely at ease.

AT YAMADA'S BIRTHDAY PARTY, I LET MYSELF DRINK quite a bit more than I should have, and by the end of the night, I was pretty drunk. Yun took it upon herself to get me back to the staff residence, where I still lived at the time. With my arm locked tightly in hers to keep my legs from buckling under me, I somehow managed to stagger up the stairs to my room.

I flopped onto the bed and she brought me a glass of water. When I emptied it in a single gulp, she refilled the glass without a word and brought it to me again. Feeling much better after the second glass, I let my head sink back onto the pillow.

Yun sat on the edge of the mattress and stroked my hair. I lay enjoying the soothing touch of her fingers, drifting in and out of a dreamworld.

After a time, I reached for her other hand and drew it to my chest, where I wrapped it gently in my own hands, slowly caressing its warmth. Lifting it to my lips, I kissed it on the back. The only illumination in the room was the light spilling from the small bedside lamp, and Yun looked prettier than ever in its soft orange glow. Her candy-drop eyes shone golden in the dim light as she gazed at me with liquid tenderness.

I tugged at her arm and motioned for her to join me in bed. She hesitated for a moment, but then timidly lay down beside me, and I wrapped my arms around her. A film of sweat made our bare skin cling. Looking up into her face, I searched her expression. I traced my finger gently over her lips as I asked, with my eyes, if I could kiss her. An almost imperceptible ripple crossed her eyes—and the reflection of myself I saw in them. I brought my face closer, as if peering into a mirror. At first our lips barely touched. The allure of Yun's face, with her downturned gaze fixed on my lips, sent a chill through me. I could barely breathe. The air between us had become thick and sultry. I slid my tongue into her mouth, drew hers into

mine, and tasted her lips. The look on her face still held a
tinge of shyness, but her tongue responded eagerly to
mine. Each time our eyes met, I could see her desire, and
she could see mine.

As we continued to kiss, I rolled over on top of her and
placed my hand on her breast. When she didn't tell me to
stop, I slipped my hand beneath her T-shirt and touched
her breast through the fabric of her bra before reaching
around behind to unhook the strap. She had adorable little breasts. Taking one in each hand, I caressed them,
blissfully losing myself in their amazing softness. I felt like
I finally knew why men are so obsessed with women's
breasts. While continuing to massage one breast with my
hand, I reached for the other with my mouth and gently
licked the nipple, drew it between my lips, and nuzzled it
with the tip of my tongue. I could feel Yun's entire body
quiver from time to time as she watched my mouth playing with her nipple.

The lusciousness of her lips and tongue gave me a sensation very nearly akin to eating—except that my stomach remained empty, and my hunger unsatisfied, no
matter how much I ate. I indulged myself greedily in the
sweetness of her mouth until my lips grew numb, and I
traced my tongue along her neck and ears as I inhaled the
smell of her skin and soaked up the warmth of her body.

"It's your first time with woman?" Yun asked in a
dreamy voice while caressing my breast.

"Yes. And you?"

"Me, too. It's first time."

"So it's the same for both of us."

"Why you do?"

"Why? Well . . . How about you?"

"I not know."

LIVING AT THE STAFF DORM POSED CERTAIN INCON-
veniences after that, so I soon moved to an apartment Yun
found for me some distance away. After I moved in, she
began staying over nearly every night.

She claimed she had been intimate with a number of
men before this, but the awkwardness of her lovemaking
betrayed her relative inexperience. It was apparently with
me that she had an orgasm for the first time, and I could
sense how deeply she was affected by it. Once she had become acquainted with the heights of ecstasy, she began
begging me for more.

And so it was that we came to share a strong physical
bond.

Making love to Yun brought me the sweetest bliss I had
ever known. I enjoyed for the first time the sensation of
truly savoring another person, and for the first time I was
overcome by a powerful desire to make someone totally
my own. It surprised me to discover that I had such a desire within me.

WE GO FOR AN EVENING DRIVE ON YUN'S YAMAHA
Sirius. It's her machine, but I'm at the handlebars this

time. Unlike my own Super Cub, which is a wheezing old man by comparison, the Sirius has plenty of power and is a much more comfortable ride. When the two of us go places together, this is the bike we take.

The most conspicuous status symbol in this country is the motorcycle a person drives, which means everybody borrows to the hilt in order to buy the most expensive machine they possibly can. Here, you're not likely to find the kind of secretly rich person you hear about every now and then in Japan, who turns out to have had a huge fortune stashed away while maintaining a modest lifestyle. In Vietnam, those who have money are eager to show off just how much they have. With so many thieves and purse snatchers prowling the city, though, you do have to be a little careful exactly how you put your wealth on display. Even when you keep your wallet in your front pocket, you'll get it swiped if you haven't pushed it far enough inside.

At this hour, the daytime slackers have recovered their energy and cruise high-spiritedly about the streets on their motorbikes. You can count on midday temperatures being blazing hot all year round, but mornings and evenings are more moderate—during the dry season, you could even say chilly. As a result, people do everything possible to avoid activity in the afternoon heat, and move about briskly during the relatively bearable morning and evening hours. They're at their best at both ends of the day, and not so much during its middle stretch.

Hai Ba Trung Street is lined with trendy boutiques

catering to the young. Clean, spacious, and brightly illu-
minated stores have T-shirts and jeans on display at upscale prices. Neatly groomed young men and women ride
up on their bikes to shop for the latest fashions. The entire
street is lit up by the flood of light spilling from the many
storefronts.

At an intersection, an old woman squats on her
haunches with a sedge hat in hand, to beg from the bikes
that sit waiting for the light to change. I see her in this
spot every night. Now and then she raises the inverted hat
to chest height and shakes it back and forth, trying to get
the motorcyclists' attention.

Twisting the throttle, I speed past a jostling pack of
bikes carrying young couples and pull ahead into the
clear. It's exhilarating to race along with the night air
rushing against my skin. I love the feeling of my long hair
trailing in the wind behind me, and I think how glad I am
that I'm not wearing a helmet.

We continue south on Hai Ba Trung until the street
bumps into the Saigon River. In this part of town you see
a lot of foreigners. Of course, I'm one of them, too, but
nobody seems to recognize me as such. Sometimes I even
get asked for directions by native Vietnamese when I'm
out on my bike.

I turn toward District 5 and drive along the river. The
breeze brings the river's sour smell, accompanied by the
strains of a pop song riding the top of the charts right
now. Directly across the water along here is District 2, in

which I have yet to set foot. Even Yun, who has lived in the city for more than twenty years, claims she's never been there. It's too dangerous, she says. I asked her once what exactly that means, when this side of the river seems plenty dangerous, too—a burglar's paradise at night, and crawling with drug addicts. Her answer, as if she'd missed the point of my question, was simply an adamant "No, no, very very dangerous! Must not go!"

Traffic is light, so I pick up my speed and feel the wind blowing even harder against my body. The later the hour, the fewer the motorcycles, but that's when the undesirables start to take over. A gang of young speed demons tears by us as if we're standing still. If they crash without helmets going that fast, they won't have a chance, I think, as I watch their taillights growing smaller and smaller in the distance.

There are so many lights in the city at night that the darkness of the sky turns pale. The moon and the stars might as well not exist. Together with the wind, time itself brushes briskly by and flows on behind me.

I don't think I've ever fully grasped that none of us has any choice but to move forward into the future. I know I should be using my eyes and mouth and ears and hands and feet and brain and every cell in my body to wake up to life's realities, but inside my head remains a blur, as if clouded by a heavy fog.

. . .

I AM DRIFTING OFF TO SLEEP IN BED WHEN MY
phone rings. It is from Japan. I've soon had all I can take
and break off the call.

"Your mother?" Yun asks with bleary eyes. She had already fallen asleep.

"Uh-huh."

"Is she well?

"Yes, yes, she's fine."

"That's good," she says contentedly, and immediately
closes her eyes again.

Hurt by Yun's naïveté, I reach under her T-shirt and
cup my hand over her petite breast. Breasts feel so good
whether you're the one touching or the one being
touched. A woman's breasts bring us a sense of security.
We all long to bury our faces in them and journey back to
childhood.

AFTER DINNER ON AN EVENING WHEN I DON'T HAVE
class, I go with Yun to visit her family. They live at the
back of a bewildering maze of alleyways, a pretty good
distance off the main street—the sort of place that takes
more than two or three trips to learn the way to by yourself. Alleys scarcely wide enough for two motorbikes to
pass are lined on both sides with homes built right up
against each other. Land is such a scarce resource here in
Ho Chi Minh City that houses are jammed together with
no spaces between.

When we arrive, Yun's mother and sisters are relaxing

in front of the TV in the living room. They're all wearing
ao ba ba. These days her mother has taken to greeting me
with a smile, but that wasn't always the case. As Yun explained to me, she developed a hatred for the Japanese
when she lived in the north, where the people suffered
from all kinds of abusive treatment under the Imperial
Japanese Army during World War II. At first I worried
about visiting, but Yun insisted it wasn't a problem, so I
kept coming along, and eventually the corners of her
mother's mouth loosened. Still, a parent's word is absolute in this country, so I'm always a little bit on edge
when I'm around her.

Yun's mother speaks Vietnamese with a northern accent. Yun herself combines both the northern and southern. She apparently switches back and forth without even
being aware of it. The whole family is Roman Catholic,
and they go to church a lot. Although I'm not religious,
they make me go with them. There are a great many
churches scattered around the city. Vietnam is said to have
the second-largest population of Christians in Southeast
Asia, after the Philippines.

The family owes a significant part of its well-being to
Yun's two older sisters living overseas—especially the sister in Australia, who not only built a home there but paid
for the family's house in Ho Chi Minh City, too. She also
put up a thousand dollars when Yun tried to launch a business several years ago. Unfortunately, the business fell
apart several months later and her thousand-dollar invest-
ment vanished into nothing. The Vietnamese are quick to

start new ventures, and their ventures frequently fail. My sense is that they neglect to do the necessary research or develop a clear business plan beforehand. Yun has tried three times to get a business off the ground, and all three times her efforts have fizzled. She lacks any kind of business sense. It's thanks only to her sister in Australia that she can afford to buy a cell phone costing several times her monthly income, or to pay cash for a motorcycle that's worth a year's salary.

Whether or not you have family living overseas has a profound effect on your standard of living in Vietnam. The family members who have earning power look after everyone else. Family is absolute. No matter what happens, family always comes first.

Yun says her mother worked herself to the bone as a peddler in order to provide for her daughters when they were growing up, pounding the pavement from early in the morning to late at night. The sisters all love their mother deeply, and they all pitch in to take care of her. They also all continue to do as their mother says.

Three of Yun's sisters—two older, one younger—share the house with Yun and her mother. Her father died many years ago, and his picture is displayed on an ancestral altar in the living room.

The fourth-oldest sister, Khanh, works for a state-run company. Even after ten years of service, she still can't get promoted. No one doubts that it's because her family didn't support the current establishment during the war. To this day, it often makes a difference which side you

were on way back then. You can't get ahead at state enter-
prises unless you have northern ties, and the national universities are said to play favorites in their admission
policies as well. Similarly, students sent by the government to study overseas all have northern roots. Not far
from the apartment building where I live is a neighborhood where great big fancy villas line the streets. I've been
told that these houses were bestowed by the government
on individuals who contributed to the northern cause in a
significant way during the war—or on their surviving
families. Yun's people are originally from the north, but
they fled the rise of communism and came south half a
century ago.

The third-oldest sister, Ngoc, is a warm, openhearted
woman, and since she's the sister Yun is closest to, she's
also the one I've gotten to know best.

Yun's younger sister, Nhung, is something of a free
spirit and not so easy to pin down. She works at the casino
inside the deluxe New World Hotel downtown. Thanks
to the tips she collects from the well-heeled clientele
there, she makes a pretty good income. Her supreme goal
in life, it seems, is to marry a foreigner; every time I see
her she wants to know if I can introduce her to someone
from Japan. She worships money. The phrase *I lo-o-ove
money* might as well be plastered across her face, and it
rolls easily off her tongue as well. She's an attractive
woman, so I imagine she must get a lot of attention from
foreign men. Her major shortcoming is that she will stop
at nothing to get what she wants.

I once entered a bar with Yun and saw Nhung behaving rather questionably with a middle-aged Asian man. As soon as she saw us, she immediately left her companion, and the bar.

"Who is that guy? That foreigner? He seems kind of creepy to me," I said to Yun.

"I not know."

"She's your little sister!"

"She's adult now, so I not say much."

Even if she's selling her body?

I realized there were family dynamics at work that an outsider, especially one from overseas, simply could not understand.

CHAPTER THREE

SUNDAY AFTERNOON, WE RIDE YUN'S Sirius south along Nam Ky Khoi Nghia Street in the blazing sunshine. Traffic is relatively light. Yesterday was hot. Today is hot. And tomorrow will be hot again. The heat is relentless every day of the year. You know this all too well, and still you can't help moaning, "Boy, it's hot," as if giving actual voice to the fact will somehow bring a small measure of relief. People do the same thing when it's cold, too—crying out "It's freezing!" to no one in particular.

The sun beats down on the asphalt roadway and on the teeming motorcycles racing along its surface. The shops and food carts lining the street, the billboards plastered with propaganda, the stagnant river emitting its noxious odors, the beggars plying the roadside—all these things that in Tokyo would appear only shabby and drab are transformed by the blinding light into objects of radiance that can be observed only through slitted eyes. A thin white veil shrouds the world around me, obscuring the boundaries between objects and making everything run together. The dazzling brightness seems to close in from all sides and give me tunnel vision.

Even though we're ten minutes late, Yun and I are the first guests to arrive at Yamada's house. The rented single-family home is located across the Saigon River in District 4; we've both been here many times before. Yamada's husband, Hieu, and their son, Dai, greet us with cheerful smiles at the door and show us into the living room. Yamada herself is busy in the adjoining kitchen and pokes her head through the door only long enough to say, "Just sit down and watch TV or something," before disappearing again.

Little Dai is keyed up and dashes about the room, squealing with excitement. Neither Yun nor I think much of Hieu, so it's hard for us to find anything to talk about. Dai's raucous behavior comes to our rescue.

Before too long, Chan and Ito arrive on Chan's motorcycle.

"Thao and Cam will be here soon, too," says Chan, who is unusually fair-skinned for a Vietnamese. "We saw them at the market up the street buying some fruit."

Ito sits down across from me.

"You came on the back of Chan's bike?" I ask him.

"Yes. She's been giving me rides a lot lately." He blushes a little.

"Normally, the man's supposed to do the driving, you know," Chan says, fixing Ito with an admonishing look through the tops of her eyes. "It's embarrassing for a man to ride behind when a woman is driving. You really need to learn!"

I detect a particular warmth in the glances going back and forth between them. Ah, so *that's* how it is between them now. I wonder when that happened.

"I can teach you," Yun says, sounding eager to do it.

"I don't know. . . . I really don't think I'm ready yet."

"You just need to take it a little at a time," I say. "Start by practicing on quiet backstreets."

"Uh-huh," he answers vaguely, obviously not at all enthusiastic about the idea.

"Hello, everybody!" Thao and Cam call out in unison as they appear in the living-room doorway. Thao is short and slim, like most Vietnamese women, but Cam is unusually tall.

"Hi! Glad you could come!" Yamada's spirited voice rings out from the kitchen. "The food's ready! Can you help me carry, Hiro?"

"I can help, too," says Chan, our youngest colleague, jumping up to follow me into the kitchen.

Thao and Cam are seasoned veterans of the language classroom, both probably around forty years old. Thao has been to Japan, and she once treated me to a dinner of the *okonomiyaki* she learned to make there. Cam often invites me to join her for dinner as well as other outings. Both women work freelance, and by all indications, they

seem to make a very good living at it. When you're a
freelancer—which is to say, when you're hired on a part-
time basis—everything rests on performance. Cam also
works as an interpreter, and her purse always seems to be
bursting with thick wads of bills.

"Cheers!" we say, lifting our voices together with our
glasses. The Vietnamese women are drinking juices and
sodas. Yamada and I have beer, and when we both down
our first glasses in a single gulp, the others respond with a
chorus of *Wow!*s.

"Ahh, somen," I say. "The refreshing lightness of the
noodles. The delectable dipping sauce. The rich savor of
genuine Japanese bonito stock. I've really missed this!"

"Eat lots," says Yamada. "I have plenty more noodles I
can boil if we need them."

I'm loving my first somen and home-style Japanese
curry in nearly two years, but gulping down too much
beer right off the bat makes me feel full, and I wind up
not being able to eat as much as I'd like. Ito, on the other
hand, displays a remarkably hearty appetite, polishing off
his curry rice in next to no time and promptly asking for
seconds. *Look at that. He can put it away after all.* Yamada
and I see it as the perfect chance to fatten him up a bit and
urge him to eat more. After taking only a single bite, Hieu
and Yun have apparently decided somen is not for them,
and they're now working silently on plates of curry.
Chan, Thao, and Cam appear to be doing fine with both
dishes. After drinking quite a few glasses of beer without

eating much food, Yamada switches to wine and urges Ito and me to join her.

"Oh, I have to tell you," she says suddenly in a loud voice. "I got my cell phone stolen yesterday."

"You did? Where?"

"Right near here. It rings while I'm driving, so I pull over to answer, but then while I'm standing there talking, this bike drives by and swipes it right out of my hand!"

"You didn't get hurt, did you?"

"No, but I'm so pissed! The thing wasn't even six months old. A five-hundred-dollar Nokia."

"What rotten luck!"

"Have you ever had anything like that happen to you?"

"No," I say. "Nobody's ever tried to steal anything from me. Not in Indonesia, not in Cambodia, and not anywhere else in Southeast Asia either. Do I really look so pathetic?"

"Hardly. But you always go local, so you blend in."

"Foreigners are definitely prime targets. You can't let your guard down for a second, or they'll get you just like that," said Thao, with a grave look. "You really have to be careful."

"Well, Yun's as local as you can get, but she's been robbed three times," I say.

"Three times?"

"Oh, don't say!" Yun protests.

"What did they take?"

"My cell phone."

"All three times?"

"Yes."

"She's just stupid," I say. "She wants to show off her fancy new phone, so she hangs it on a lanyard around her neck for everybody to see. That's practically asking for somebody to grab it, right? Even us outsiders can see that."

"That's not true," Yun says. "Before I drive, I put into my shirt."

"But somebody still just grabbed the lanyard, and that was it. A three-hundred-dollar Sony Ericsson. You're just not thinking."

"You're mean, Hiro."

"The way they pulled it off, with perfect timing, they had to be professionals. Two guys on a motorbike. The one on the back did the work."

Stolen phones are sold openly on the street and in shops as used equipment.

"But one time I win," Yun says.

"What do you mean?"

"Somebody try to steal my bag, so his motorbike, I kick hard. The thief is very surprised, and he run away."

"Ooh! You showed that guy!"

"What about you, Thao? Have you ever had anything stolen?"

"I don't think so," says Thao. "Oh, wait, there was this one time when somebody swiped a hat right off my head."

"Wow, so everybody has stories like that," I say. "That's kind of scary! I guess I should be more careful."

WHEN EVERYONE'S HAD ALL THE NOODLES AND CURRY they want, Thao begins cutting open the fruit she picked up on her way here.

"Oh, goodie! You brought durians," Yamada says. She is extremely fond of this "king of fruits."

"But you can't mix durian with alcohol."

Yamada groans. "That's right! I've been drinking, so I guess I have to pass!"

"Maybe you should try some anyway. See what happens," I say, grinning mischievously.

"What's the worst that can happen? It kills me?" Yamada asks, with a big, drunken smile.

"Yes," says Yun. "It kill you."

"That's right," the others chime in. "It really can kill you. It's very dangerous. You mustn't have any."

"Ooo-kay," Yamada says. "In that case, I'll stick to pomelo." She downs the rest of her wine before rising unsteadily to her feet and going into the kitchen mumbling, "Munchies, munchies."

Hieu quietly nurses his beer as he keeps Dai occupied, occasionally exchanging a few words with Cam and the others. It appears Ito can't handle too much alcohol: a single glass of beer and a single glass of wine have turned his face a bright crimson. Nothing is slowing me down yet, and Yun scolds that I shouldn't drink so much. She casts dirty looks my way as she chews on pieces of durian, which is one of her favorite fruits, too.

The Vietnamese are extremely fond of durian. When it's fresh, the fruit doesn't have the terrible smell it's famous for, but even then the creamy flesh is too rich and heavy for my taste. I feel pretty much the same way about jackfruit. Basically, my stomach does not take kindly to the heavy richness that is so typical of tropical fruits. They have a potency far beyond the satsumas and sand pears and apples that are our staples in Japan.

Yamada returns bearing cheese and crackers and chips. She's in a feisty mood.

"Come on, drink up," she says to Ito, noticing his half-full glass.

"Thanks, but I'm afraid I'm really not much of a drinker. . . ."

"Yeah, yeah, yeah, never mind that," she says, topping the glass off all the way to the brim. She takes the opportunity to fill my glass as well. I feel the sting of Yun's glare.

The conversation among our Vietnamese colleagues has turned to Japanese study, and I hear Yun asking Cam about the best methods. The party has naturally divided into two separate groups along national lines—the drunken Japanese and the sober local folks.

"So I guess you patched things up with your husband?" I say to Yamada.

"Basically, yeah," she says, hiccuping. "It all comes down to love in the end, you know. Love."

"Love? . . . I see," I say, trying not to sound too dubious. *What can she possibly see to love in that little boy of a man? I guess they must have their own private little world that no one else sees or understands.*

"Don't you have anybody, Hiro?"

"Huh?" I'm thrown by the unexpected question. "Oh. No, nobody."

"Are you su-u-ure?" She waggles the glass in her right hand and gives me a look that says she's not going to let me get off easy. She could be trouble, this woman.

I turn to Ito, in an effort to move the conversation away from me. "You're single, right?"

"Yes, at heart," he mumbles, almost inaudibly, pushing his glasses up with his index finger. His face is as red as boiled octopus.

Not sure that I've heard correctly, I ask, "Excuse me? What'd you just say?"

"Yes, um . . . that is . . . well . . . actually, no, I'm not single," he says feebly, taking a sip of wine. His eyes are bloodshot and bleary.

"You're joking! You're really not?" Yamada and I raise our voices in disbelief.

"Right . . . that is . . . um . . ." he mumbles under his breath, keeping his eyes averted. I wait for what will come next, but he sits there taking sips of his wine in silence and gives no indication he's about to say anything more.

Realizing I've stumbled onto an unwelcome topic, I struggle to think of something else more agreeable to talk about. Just as I'm about to open my mouth again, Yamada takes a different tack.

"So you're saying you have a wife back in Japan?" she asks bluntly.

"Yes, sort of." He removes his glasses and begins wiping the lenses with a handkerchief he fishes from his pocket. He's one of those people who looks good in glasses but kind of goofy without.

"Single at heart?" Yamada's tone always tends to become more forceful when she's drunk, and now there's a distinct edge to it.

"Um, yes . . . it's a long story. . . . We were actually supposed to get divorced before I came to Vietnam, but things got a little complicated." Replacing his freshly cleaned glasses on his nose, he looks at me as he speaks, even though it was Yamada who asked the question. A burst of laughter rises from the other group. I glance over and my eyes meet Yun's. She gives me a wink.

"Do you have any children?" Yamada is starting to sound like an interrogator.

"Yes, one girl," he says after an uncomfortable pause.

"How old?"

"Eight." His answer comes more crisply this time, as if he's finally realized there's no use trying to hold anything back.

"Men who have no sense of responsibility are the lowest of the low," Yamada says disdainfully.

I don't like the direction this is taking. "I think maybe you've had enough," I say, snatching Yamada's glass away from her. "You're getting belligerent."

"Hey! Give that back!" She reaches for the glass in my hand.

"So I suppose you're saying that your own husband has the proper sense of responsibility?" Ito glares at her contentiously. It's the first time I've ever seen him be so assertive.

"Yes, he does! He does! He does!" Yamada shouts, sounding very much as though she's actually trying to convince herself. She grabs the wineglass back from me and promptly drains its contents.

Really? I can't say it looks that way to me. And I'm pretty sure everyone else in this room besides herself and her son would agree. None of them would ever say so to her face, but they all assume Hieu married her only for her money. Thao and the others worry about her and take advantage of occasions like this to come and look in on her now and then. As a matter of fact I imagine Yamada herself begrudgingly suspects the same, more than a little; she simply can't bring herself to admit it.

"My wife ran off with another man," Ito says softly, a smile tugging at his lips, as he refills Yamada's glass. "It happens all the time."

"Oh!" Yamada looks as if she has instantly been shaken sober. "I'm sorry. I didn't—"

"Please think nothing of it," he cuts her off. "I don't let

it bother me." The smile that spreads across his face looks completely genuine.

We quietly sip our wine for a few moments, saying nothing. The lively banter and laughter from the other group makes our silence feel even worse. Finally I can bear the awkward lull no longer.

"Well, I guess life serves up all kinds. All kinds of men, and all kinds of women, too. How about we leave it at that and go out for some karaoke?" I suggest, straining to change the mood.

To my surprise, Yamada immediately perks up and cries, "Great idea! Let's go! Let's go!" Then she turns to the others and announces, "Listen up, everybody! We're going to karaoke!"

"Is there someplace nearby that has Japanese songs?"

"I don't know about around here, but Karaoke Nice in District One has some," Cam says.

"That seems kinda far. Though it's fine for the rest of us since it's on our way home."

"Don't worry about that. Hieu hasn't had that much to drink, so I'll make him drive. Right?" she says, turning to her husband. He nods back vaguely.

AT THE KARAOKE HOUSE, YAMADA CONTINUES DRINK-ing like a fish as she enthusiastically belts out songs from Japan and Vietnam. She's partying the way middle-aged men do back in Japan. Yun finally puts her foot down and makes me switch to juice. Ito drinks some more, but then nods off at one end of the sofa. Chan casts a concerned eye his way from time to time, a fact that is not lost on Thao or Cam.

Noticing the two of them watching Chan, Yamada says under her breath so only I can hear, "They both had their eyes on him, too."

Yun has launched into a martial song. To be perfectly honest, she's not much of a singer.

"You're kidding! Really?"

"Basically, they're all looking to snag a Japanese husband, you know. But Chan's younger and prettier, so of course the man's going to choose her."

"Wow, I had no idea."

"You're so dense sometimes, Hiro. But Japanese men sure do have it good, don't they? Being so popular."

"I'd say Japanese women seem pretty popular, too."

"Then why don't I see a boyfriend on your arm?"

"Vietnamese men aren't my type. Oh, except Lam Truong. He's definitely hot."

Lam Truong is one of Vietnam's most popular singers.

"Lam Truong? I think he's an ethnic Chinese, right? So maybe that's what you need to look for."

"I don't really think that's the issue."

"How do you ever expect to get married if you keep saying things like that?"

"That's okay. I don't really want to get married. Oh, it's your turn next."

When Yun hands her the microphone, Yamada stands
and begins singing Saki Kubota's "The Stranger." Older
songs like that seem to be her forte.

"Why do you all like martial songs so much?" I ask Yun.

"Martial songs?"

"Songs about war."

"They make you energy. *Rum pa pum pum!*" she says.
"Music is very good. But words is not so good. About war.
About big suffering."

"Which war are they about?"

"France. And America."

Our karaoke party goes on for three more hours before
finally breaking up. I'm still a little wobbly so I let Yun do
the driving.

Once we are alone, she says, "Yamada-san drink so
much. Drink like man." She sounds genuinely appalled.
"And today you drink too much, too," she adds, casting a
troubled look over her shoulder.

"Watch the road," I tell her. "I don't see why it's a problem if it's just sometimes."

"It's dangerous."

"You don't need to worry. Did you get a chance to talk
to Hieu today?"

"Only a little. He not very good man. Why Yamada-san
marry him?"

"I suppose because she loves him."

"But she is pretty. She can marry Japanese man."

"I don't think she likes Japanese men very much."

"Same like you, yes? Last boyfriend not Japanese, yes?"

"The one before that was Japanese."

"Why you say goodbye to last boyfriend?"

"Because he went back home to his own country."

"That means, when you go home to Japan, you say goodbye to me?"

"Even if I do go home to Japan, I don't want to say goodbye to you," I reply. "How about you?"

"If you go to stay in Japan, I become very lonely. I not want you to go."

"You want me to live in Vietnam forever?"

"Yes. Live in Vietnam, and go home sometimes."

"Let's ride a little more. Take the riverfront road."

"Riverfront?"

"Along the river. The road along the river."

"Oh, I see. Riverfront road. Riverfront road. I learn it."

"Very good."

Yun giggles. I pull myself tight against her diminutive back and nuzzle up to her neck, inhaling the smell of her skin.

As usual, no stars are visible in the sky above. The slight chill in the night air is perfect for clearing the haze of alcohol from my head.

I wonder: When people grow old, do those who say they were happily married outnumber those who never were?

What *is* marriage anyway?

CHAPTER FOUR

AS I'M FINISHING UP AT WORK AND preparing to leave for the day, Yamada comes hurrying in from her last class and stops me.

"I have this thing I have to go to, and I don't want to go alone, so I need you to come with me. Okay? Please?"

"What kind of thing?"

"A party."

"With who?"

"It'll be mainly Japanese businessmen and their wives. I say party, but basically it's just drinks and dinner."

"I think I'll pass."

But as I start to turn away, she grabs my right arm.

"You don't have class tonight, do you?"

"No. Why?"

"Well, I was asked by one of our clients, so this is part

of the job. I expect your cooperation." This time she sounds like a boss issuing an order to her subordinate.

"Wha-a-at?" I protest. "You're abusing your authority!"

"Come on, Hiro. I'm a friend in need. Help me out here." Now she's trying to guilt me into it.

"I'd like to, I really would, but there are certain things a person knows she's just not cut out for."

"It won't be that bad. We really only have to put in an appearance. We'll have a little to eat and drink, and then we can leave. Okay? Please? I'm begging you, Hiro."

"All right. Fine. I'll go."

The party is at a French restaurant that's been rented out for the evening. I notice instantly as we enter that the other women have all dressed for the occasion. Since I've come straight from the office in my work clothes, I feel like turning on my heels and walking right back out.

As I had anticipated, once we're inside I feel as though I'm back in Japan. People are amazed that we rode over on motorcycles. Everybody else there is used to being chauffeured everywhere in a company car or gets around by taxi.

The men are all talking about business and the women are gossiping about cooking classes, hotel gyms, and travel. I'm reminded that it's because I hate having to make small talk like this that I've so often chosen to enjoy my own company instead. Keeping empty conversation going is an exhausting exercise.

I can tell from the things they say that most of these people see themselves as at least a step or two above the

Vietnamese. And I suppose they look down on me in
much the same way. I can't help wondering how this
makes Yamada feel, but she seems oblivious to any such
attitudes as she discusses business with the client who
asked her here. This client is the only person in the room
besides me who knows that she is half Vietnamese.

I settle into an inconspicuous spot in the corner and
look around the room. It's hard to tell from the expres-
sions on people's faces whether they are enjoying themselves or not. I do sense a very complicated web of
friendships and relationships at play. In particular, there
appears to be a subtle hierarchy at work within the micro-
cosm of Japanese society present in the room. The over-
powering smell of Japan makes me want to gasp for air.
It's been a long while since I've felt so utterly uncomfortable in a place. I can't imagine ever wanting to become a
part of this group.

I'm getting ready to claim that I have another commit-
ment and excuse myself when a man comes up to me and
asks, "So what exactly do you ride?"

He's a large man with a dark tan who looks like the ath-
letic type. There's some color in his cheeks, no doubt
from having had a few. I can't immediately think who he
reminds me of.

"A Honda Super Cub."

"Think maybe I could see what it's like?"

He's grinning like a child who's just thought up some
new piece of mischief. *Who does he remind me of?*

"Sure. Do you mean right now? Here, I'll give you the key, and the parking ticket. Be my guest."

"Oh, but I couldn't possibly drive in this city."

"Huh?"

"You have to drive," he says.

Oh, now I know who.

"You mean you want me to drive and you'll ride on the back?"

"That's right." He smiles cheerfully. "What do you say?"

Tetsuya. He reminds me of Tetsuya.

"Well, I guess, but . . ."

I look at him. He's a big guy and I wonder if it's such a good idea. The only passengers I've ever carried on the back of my bike were all much lighter.

"All right!" he exclaims. "Just a little ride is all I'm asking. Later on."

"Later on?"

"Uh-huh. Is that a problem?"

"In that case, maybe I can just drive you home?"

"Oh? You wouldn't mind?"

I keep looking at him and thinking of Tetsuya. Tetsuya was one of my mother's many lovers—uncharacteristically young and good-looking for her. She was with him for about a year, if I remember correctly. As usual, she got dumped in the end. My seventeenth birthday came while they were together, and he gave me a present—a teddy bear, wrapped in paper that was plastered with cartoon characters and tied with a shocking pink ribbon. It devastated me to be treated so completely like a child. I'd have preferred to think of him as boyfriend material rather than a father figure.

"Where do you live?" I ask.

"On Le Thanh Ton."

"That's not far at all. You can easily walk it."

"But they say it's not safe to be out on foot at night. Oh, sorry, I never introduced myself. My name is Konno."

He hands me his business card.

"An importer?"

"Basically."

"I'm Hiromi Azuma."

"And you teach Japanese?"

"Yes."

"That's amazing."

"What do you mean?"

As we continue to chat, I realize that he's talking to me in a distinctly different way from any of the others I've spoken to here. I obviously don't belong in this crowd, and yet he keeps asking one question after another as if he's genuinely curious about my life. He urges me to eat and drink some more as he tells me about his work and other activities with a carefree smile. I can tell he's trying to put me at ease. He must have seen me looking bored in the corner and decided to come to my rescue. Which was very nice of him, I think to myself. I learn that he's ten years older than me and unmarried.

"You mean, without any divorces?"

"That's right."

"What have you been doing with your time?"

"Working. How about you? Were you married before?"

"No."

"So what have you been doing with *your* time, then?"

"Studying."

"Are we stupid, you think?"

"Hardly."

He tells me he's been so busy with work since arriving in Vietnam two months ago that he's barely had time to catch his breath. Waves of nostalgia wash over me as I observe him. I find myself wondering what Tetsuya might be up to now, all these years later, and it triggers conflicting emotions inside me. One moment I want to talk with Konno all the more, and the next I want to push him away.

WE RIDE TOGETHER FROM THE RESTAURANT TO THE luxury condominium building where Konno lives. My Super Cub groans under his weight. Konno, who is one of those who normally go everywhere by taxi, pretends to be worried, but I can tell he's actually amused.

"Think we might blow a tire?"

"I got a brand-new one when I had a flat recently, so we should be fine."

"Are you sure?"

The motorbike wobbles under the extra weight, and I have to put all my strength into steering in a straight line.

We reach his building in no time. Built with foreign residents in mind, it resembles a fancy hotel.

"Wow!" I say, gazing up at the structure. "This looks really posh. It must be nice inside."

"It's very comfortable. You'll have to come up sometime."

I'm not sure how to respond.

"What's the matter?" he says.

"What do you mean?"

"Your face went stiff."

"Huh? No way. It did not."

I instinctively raise both hands to my cheeks. Konno chuckles.

"Are you free tomorrow night?" he asks.

"Tomorrow? I teach until nine."

"You work that late?"

"When I have an evening class."

"How about the day after?"

"The day after . . . I'm done around six."

"Then come pick me up at my office when you're through. The address is on my card. You seem to know your way around so I'm sure you can find it. I'll treat you to dinner. And you can give me another ride on your bike."

"Okay," I say, a little uncertainly.

"Good night, then. Drive carefully."

Konno walks briskly into the building, past the doorman on duty. All in all, he seems like a cheerful guy, but I've also noticed a look that suggests sadness cross his face from time to time. I stand there wondering what to make of my first brush with masculinity in ages and the fond memories it has awakened.

Several years after Tetsuya left my mother, I bumped into him one day in Shinjuku Station. This time he treated me like a grown woman. It was an odd feeling to become the object of romantic advances from a man who'd once acted like a father to me—treating me like a child and showing no interest in me. We dated for a while after that, but as his passion grew more heated, mine cooled down. In the end, I broke it off. I felt as though I'd beaten my mother in a contest.

TWO DAYS LATER, I GO TO PICK KONNO UP AT HIS OF-fice as agreed. It is on the twelfth floor of an ultramodern high-rise. When I poke my head in the door, I see that he's the only person there.

"Did everybody else go home already?"

"Uh-huh. Though, of course, besides me, they're all Vietnamese. Just three of them. It's like this every day. I'm the only one who works late. I'm the only one who works on Sunday, too."

I get the feeling things aren't going particularly well with his staff.

Konno speaks no Vietnamese, and his English is only fair. One of his employees speaks rudimentary English and middling Japanese; the other two speak decent English but no Japanese. Under the circumstances, I'm impressed that he manages to get anything done at all. There has to be a fair amount of miscommunication that's frustrating to deal with.

He seems worn out from coping with the demands of his job in this strange land.

"Sounds like things have been pretty tough for you. Are you holding up all right?" I ask him.

"Yeah. I'm holding up like shit," he cracks, and I'm not quite sure how to take it.

As I interact with Konno, I feel as though I'm realizing for the first time that men and women are altogether different creatures. I sense how essentially unalike we are—from the shape and constitution of our bodies to the way our minds work. In his presence, I become intensely aware that I am a woman. Men and women give off entirely different smells. When I get a whiff of Konno's scent, it sets something inside me trembling, but I can't decide whether it's a good feeling or a bad one.

I CONTINUE SEEING KONNO FROM TIME TO TIME. Yun is quick to notice and soon finds ways to disrupt our meetings.

One evening, I'm out with Konno at a nightclub on the top floor of a downtown hotel. A female vocalist of indeterminate nationality is singing a soft English tune accompanied by a relatively subdued backup band. Apart from the two of us, the place is filled with Westerners, and the tables in the room buzz with conversation. I am sipping a

red cocktail, Konno a gin and tonic. As he sits with his
back to the window, my eyes are drawn to his broad, muscular shoulders silhouetted against the nightscape of the
city, and to his thick, strong hand resting on the table.

Each time our eyes meet, his gaze sends a little quiver
through me. No doubt my own eyes sparkle flirtatiously
in return. It's a conditioned response.

We've had several rounds and I'm starting to feel mel-
low when my phone rings.

"Hello?"

It's Yun. "What time you go home tonight?" she says.

"Um, I don't really know."

"Night is dangerous, so go home early please. I go
there too and wait."

"All right. Fine."

"And no alcohol."

Too late. I'm already drinking.

"Sure, fine, talk to you later," I say, and click off before
she can say anything more.

"Was that Yun?" Konno inquires stiffly. It's easy for him
to guess, because she makes a point of calling every time
I'm with him.

"She thinks I should head home before it's too late," I
say, forcing a smile.

"You're really tight, aren't you, the two of you? Like a
couple of sweethearts," he says. His face is unreadable. I
was afraid we might give that impression.

"We've gotten to be like family," I say, trying to pass it
off. "Though I suppose it might seem a little strange."

Konno says little more after that, and soon he considerately suggests that we call it a night. I was actually wishing I could stay with him a little longer.

When I get back to the apartment, Yun is stretched out on the bed watching TV.

"Did you have dinner?" I ask, lying down next to her. I place my hand on her stomach and begin rubbing it back and forth.

"No," she says. Her face is wooden, and she keeps her eyes on the TV.

"Why in the world not?"

"Because you not here."

"Then why don't you just eat with your family?" I'm getting annoyed.

"You drink?" she asks.

"No."

"Yes, you drink. I can tell."

"Only a little."

"You have good time? Konno-san is well?"

"He seemed tired."

"That's too bad," she says, and buries her face in my chest. She seems to be coming out of her sulk because I came home early. "I'm hungry."

"Shall we go out?"

"Do you love me, Hiro?"

"Yes, I love you."

"Truly?"

"Yes. Truly."

"Make noodles for me."

"Ramen again? Really?"

"Please," she says, looking at me with puppy-dog eyes.

"Fine, fine. So all I have to do is boil water."

She giggles. "I love you, Hiro," she says, and a little bashfully she kisses me on the cheek. She's so endearing when she's this way. I realize that Konno is beginning to fade from the place he's held in my consciousness.

Virtually this same sequence of events occurs over and over again.

ONE EVENING YUN AND I HEAD TO A SHOPPING CENTER that includes a superstore, several boutiques, a couple of shoe stores, a bookstore, a bakery, a KFC franchise, and a video arcade all in one building. There are a number of these places scattered around the city, each filled with different supermarkets and retail tenants. Since I lived for a long time in the midst of Tokyo's inundation of shops and highly developed consumer culture, coming to one of these complexes makes me feel right at home. We walk up and down the aisles, throwing bags of coffee beans, toilet paper, body wash, snack foods, and so on into our cart.

"Let's eat at apartment tonight. I cook. What you want to eat?" Yun asks.

"Clams. Let's have clams."

"Okay. And shrimp, too. We can buy later at market."

We get all our perishable foods at our nearby market rather than the superstore. The food there is not only cheaper but fresher.

In the women's clothing section, a rack of camisole dresses intended as loungewear catches my eye. There's a selection of bright colors with pretty flower patterns.

"Isn't this cute?" I say, holding a pink one up in front of Yun.

"I not wear."

Yun always dresses like a boy.

"But it's adorable. I'm gonna buy it. I want you to wear it. Okay?"

"What?" she protests. "I am too embarrassed!"

"No, no, you'll look cute."

WE PROCEED TO THE MARKET AND PICK UP TWO kilos of shrimp and three kilos of something that looks sort of halfway between the common orient clam and Japanese littlenecks. Shellfish are hauled into Ho Chi Minh City from the Mekong Delta on a daily basis. We also buy three kilos of fruit while we're there. The motorcycle is loaded to capacity, with our purchases balanced between my legs, dangling from Yun's hands and both handlebars, and sandwiched between my back and her stomach as I start unsteadily for home.

"Be careful," Yun says. "Go slowly."

"Don't worry. You know I'm a good driver. Right?"

"Yes, yes. In front. Look in front."

Back at the apartment, Yun immediately starts cooking. The clams she simply simmers with some spices in
coconut water, the shrimp with some spices in beer.
When the food is ready she sets the pan with the clams
right on the table, and we grab the shells with our fingers
one after the other to eat them. The meat is plump and
tender, with just the right amount of saltiness to keep you
coming back for more. The clams and shrimp alone are
plenty to fill us up, without any rice.

"They're good, aren't they?"

"*Ngon qua* (They're super good)."

"I wonder if we can eat them all."

"Let's invite Tan-san and Bao-san," she says and jumps
up to go out into the hall.

Tan lives in the unit to my left, and Bao in the one to
my right. Tan is a single woman my own age who works
in the accounting department of the company Yun works
for. It was through her that Yun found this apartment for
me. Tan spends hours every evening at an Internet café.
According to Yun, she's been boasting that she found an
American boyfriend on the Web who sends her money
even though they've never actually met. I have no idea
what that means.

Bao works in the office at Thai Air, speaks Thai, and
has a Thai boyfriend. She's twenty-five years old and ex-
traordinarily attractive. Her door is often propped wide
open when I go by, and I see her lounging around in her
underwear, or she'll come up to me, obviously braless, in
a thin white tank top, making me feel as though I ought to

cover my eyes. When she's talking on the phone in Thai
with her boyfriend, all the *caw* sounds make me think of a
crow. By comparison, the incomprehensible Vietnamese I
hear around town is punctuated with frequent *nyar*s that
sound more like a cat. This makes me wonder what Japanese sounds like to people who don't speak the language.
Since it's my mother tongue, there's simply no way I can
hear it as empty sound. But I imagine it must sound
pretty funny when it comes from somebody who likes to
use a lot of onomatopoeic and mimetic words—all those
*piko-piko*s and *bata-bata*s and *nyoki-nyoki*s. Japanese people
tend to speak English with a kind of bounciness, so does
that mean our whole language sounds that way to others?
Like bouncing over bumps?

"*Tan oi! Bao oi!*" Yun's voice echoes down the hall.

There are two additional apartments on this floor—
one occupied by two sisters who are college students, the
other by a guy about the same age. Every once in a while
I see this guy in Bao's room. He'll be sitting side by side
with the scantily clad Bao on her bed, watching TV. I'm
not sure what that means either.

"Both not here," Yun comes back to report.

"How about the college students?"

"They go home yesterday. Visiting parents."

"Then I guess we'll just have to find room in our own
bellies."

Yun is an insatiable seafood lover. She begins tossing
clams and shrimp into her mouth again at a rapid pace.

When she's done, she flops back onto the tile floor and exclaims, "*No roi. No roi.* (I'm stuffed)."

"We actually ate them all, didn't we?" I say.

"Yes, we did."

"Let me see your tummy, Yun."

She laughs. Yun's stomach after a meal is a sight to behold. A pronounced mound appears beneath her petite little breasts. I gently pass my hand across her belly, gazing admiringly at its marvelous bulge.

"It's like you're expecting."

"Expecting?"

"Expecting a child," I explain. "It's like you're going to have a baby."

"No baby!"

After finishing my last few bites, I stretch out on the floor beside her. A quiz show Yun likes comes on the tube, and she curls forward to watch. I watch from where I lie, eating some mangosteen.

Yun pops a peachy white piece of mangosteen into her mouth, then licks the juice from each of her fingertips.

The outer rind of a mangosteen is dark, hard, and dry, but hidden inside is a moist white flesh. Each time I crack one open, my heart races as if I'm looking at something I'm not supposed to see. The fruit's fresh, sweet smell fills me with a feeling of abundance.

"Could you cut these?" I say, holding out the two green mangos we bought at the same time as the mangosteens.

When they're green, mangos are hard and not yet

sweet. They have a crisp-crunchy texture, and the custom
is to treat them more like a vegetable than a fruit, flavor-
ing them with a mixture of red pepper and salt and sugar.
Yun deftly slices up the mangos into bite-sized pieces in
the palm of her hand and passes them back to me.

We lie across from each other on the floor, munching
on mangos and mangosteens with our eyes glued to the
TV. The quiz show pits regular people against each other
under the same rules and on virtually the same studio set
as a show I used to watch in Japan, so each time I watch, I
feel a sense of déjà vu. The only differences are the nationality of the contestants and the language they speak.
Yun shouts out the answers before the contestants on the
screen, then cheers or groans, depending on whether she
got the answer right.

When the show is over, she lets out a big yawn, lies
back, and stretches her arms and legs wide. I lay my head
sideways on the mound of her stomach, which is already
beginning to subside, and my ear fills with the sounds of
her digestive system at work. I start to crack up.

"What?" says Yun with a bemused grin.

"Your stomach's making these amazing noises. *Burble
burble burble.*"

She giggles.

I keep my ear pressed to her belly for a while, letting
out a string of *Ooh!*s and *Wow!*s.

"What about you?" Yun finally says, and presses her ear
to my stomach. "Yes, your stomach make noise, too. *Glub-
a-glub-a-glub.*"

"*Glub-a-glub?*"

I gently stroke Yun's head on my stomach. Her hair feels dried out, both from too much sun and from being chemically bleached.

"I'm tired today," Yun sighs.

"Oh! You need to try on that camisole dress," I say, suddenly remembering.

"No. You try on."

"It's not big enough for me. Here. Put it on."

I pull the dress from the shopping bag and break off the tag before giving it to her. She seems to move in slow motion as she begins changing, but I don't get the sense that she's especially reluctant.

"How you think?" she asks when she's put it on, striking a pose a little sheepishly. The shocking pink goes well with her lustrous, light brown skin.

"See, I told you it'd be cute. It flatters you. It's adorable."

Yun giggles. "You like?"

"Yes."

"How much?"

"As much as all of Vietnam."

"Wow! All of Vietnam!"

Yun smiles, as if she's the happiest girl in the world. Sometimes this simple childlike innocence makes my heart just melt. I let her put her head in my lap and I stroke her hair.

"You are very pretty, Hiro," she says, looking up at me.

She takes my right hand and gently folds it between her

own at her chest. Her small, warm fingers begin slowly, tenderly caressing mine. It turns me on when Yun plays with my hand like this. She continues to stroke back and forth, never stopping, moving endlessly from one finger to the next. With a smile, she lifts my hand to her lips and kisses it, then closes her eyes.

Every so often, a breath of wind from outside ruffles the lace curtains. I sit quietly, enjoying the brush of air against my cheek from the electric fan, feeling the coolness of the floor beneath my legs, and listening to the distant buzz of motorcycle engines and the calls of street vendors drifting in through the window, and I feel utterly at peace.

YUN AND I ARE SOUND ASLEEP IN BED WHEN A SUDden furious pounding at the door jolts us awake. I switch on the light and look at my watch. It's past midnight. Yun goes to open the door. I hear her talking to my landlord. It sounds serious.

"The police are here," she says, rushing back to me.

"Oh, shit. What should I do? Are they going to take me to the police station?"

"No worries. I go now and talk to them. You wait here. I need money please."

"Oh, right, a bribe. Or sorry, I mean coffee money. You need coffee money. How much?" I ask. "I'm counting on you, Yun."

"No worries. You wait here."

She and the landlord are jabbering back and forth about something as they start down the stairs.

So they've finally come after me. It had to happen eventually. I've lived in this building for more than a year and a half, trying not to attract attention so the authorities wouldn't realize I'm a foreigner living in unlicensed accommodations, but somebody must have tipped them off.

Yun and my landlord take care of things with the officers for the moment and that is the end of it for tonight. But the stipulation is that I have to move out within a week.

"How about where Kanazawa-san live?" Yun asks.

"I was thinking of that, too. That would be the easiest, wouldn't it? Especially since it's so close. Could you go ask them tomorrow if they have any vacancies, and also how much the rent would be?"

"Okay."

I exhale loudly. "Whew, what a scare, though! The police!"

"I scared, too. But everything turn out no problem. Very easy."

"It's lucky that you have friends who are cops. And that you're such a good talker. You're the best, Yun. What would I do in this country without you? Thank you."

She just giggles.

When her high-school-age nephew came home from Australia for a visit, he got into a fight with some local boys. Yun and I both happened to be there at the time, and she immediately called one of her friends on the police force to ask for help. Four officers were on the scene in less than five minutes. They all appeared to be about my own age, and they were terrifically good-looking as well.

Everybody in this country trembles before the police. The police represent absolute power. They're much more intimidating than law enforcement in Japan. They keep close tabs on who lives where within their jurisdiction. Anytime you move, you have to report your new address to them, and they even know whether you sympathized with the North or the South during the war.

THE NEXT DAY WE GO TO SEE THE PLACE WHERE Kanazawa lives, just three doors down from Hai's café. It's a huge four-story house, with the second, third, and fourth floors divided into four apartments each. Kanazawa lives on the top floor. Nearly half of the units are vacant.

The apartments are basically single rooms with attached baths, and I instantly fall in love with the most spacious one on the third floor. It has big French windows that open onto a balcony and it gets plenty of light. The ceiling fan and the bathroom fixtures are all very ornate, reminding me of a hotel. I wince a little when I hear the rent, which is four times what I've been paying, but I'm getting a little tired of living so frugally, and looking for something cheaper seems like too much of a hassle, so I decide right then and there to take it. I'll even have access to the spacious roof, which looks like it will be a great place to relax.

I wait until the weekend to move. Kanazawa pitches in, too. That night, Yun and I have dinner with Kanazawa, as well as the building caretaker, Cham, and her two young sons. Cham welcomes us warmly. She's my own age and divorced. Because she's originally from the ancient city of Hue in central Vietnam, she has a heavy accent and often speaks in a dialect that I don't understand. Even Yun has difficulty following what she's saying and has to ask her to repeat things sometimes. To me it sounds like an entirely different language. Once she realizes that I can't understand her, she makes an effort to speak in the Saigon dialect. Her boys are big fans of *The Gao Rangers* from Japan, and they keep asking me to tell them what the characters are saying in Japanese as they watch a VCD.

Cham needs my passport in order to file the proper residency report with the police, so I give it to her.

"I was surprised when Satoshi's passport wasn't Japanese," she says, using Kanazawa's given name. "Even though he speaks Japanese."

"It's not? So what country are you from?" I ask him.

"I'm Korean. Didn't I ever tell you?"

"This is the first I'm hearing of it."

"But I'm a permanent resident of Japan."

"Now that you mention it, there's a lot of people like you here, aren't there?"

"I can't say that I've noticed."

"Do you speak Korean?" I ask.

"Uh-uh."

"Not at all?"

"Nope."

"And that's okay?"

"Sure. Believe it or not, I was a youth leader in Mindan back in Japan," he tells me.

"What's Mindan?"

"It's an organization for resident Koreans."

"Oh yeah?"

"Listen to you. If you're teaching the language, shouldn't you know something like that?"

"Ouch. You hit on a sore spot there."

"If you Korean," Yun says, "why you not speak Korean?"

"Because I was born and raised in Japan."

"So you speak only Japanese?"

"That's right."

"But you belong to Korea?"

"Uh-huh."

"It's very strange, I think."

"Satoshi needs girlfriend," Cham interjects, grinning widely. "Maybe can you introduce him someone?"

Whether he's Japanese or Korean, he's a foreigner either way, so you'd normally expect the local girls to be pursuing him right and left.

"Could it be your standards are too high?" I ask him.

"No, no. You know how the girls here all have these *Pretty Woman* fantasies? Well, that's a problem for me—

that whole mind-set. Because I want to be the one getting taken care of. Any idea where I can find that girl? The one who'll wait on me hand and foot? The one who'll tell me I don't have to do a damn thing."

"I doubt she exists," I say after a pause.

"Oh, I promise you she exists."

"Well, in that case, good luck finding her. You're on your own."

"Actually, I had someone like that in Thailand."

"So, what happened?"

"We broke up."

"A rare catch like that, why didn't you hang on to her?"

"Well, you know, people's feelings are like bubbles on water. So it's tough. Things get complicated."

"Bubbles on water . . . ?"

I figure the chances are pretty high that Kanazawa is actually gay.

"By the way, if you'd like to borrow any of my books," he says, "I'll be happy to lend them to you. So long as you promise to bring them back."

He has a sizable collection of Japanese books, which I've come to refer to as the Kanazawa Library. Some of them he brought with him from Japan, and others he picked up during his stay in Thailand. Since Japanese books are hard to come by in this country, I'm grateful for his offer.

The bulk of the Kanazawa Library is made up of novels, but he also has a fair number of books by Takeshi Kaiko, Katsuichi Honda, Bun'yo Ishikawa, Taizo Ichinose, and Kyoichi Sawada—all well known for their coverage of the Vietnam War.

I was born in the year the war ended, and it represents no more than a distant echo to me. But I do know that military planes took off for Vietnam from bases in Japan, and procurements for the war enriched the Japanese economy. Japan's economic growth was founded in a very real sense on events that occurred here. So I cannot claim that I have no connection to them.

WHEN SHE HEARS THAT KANAZAWA PLANS TO VISIT the War Remnants Museum, Yun declares immediately that she will be his guide—even though he never asked. Since she's in the process of studying to be a tour guide, she apparently sees it as an opportunity to get some practice.

"That's okay. This is actually my second visit. I don't really need a guide," he says, but she pays no attention.

I know it'll be an interesting excursion, so I decide to tag along. One of the best-known tourist spots in Ho Chi Minh City, the museum is home to a wealth of information about the Vietnam War—called the American War here. Among the items on display are actual fighter planes and tanks, replicas of tiger cages and execution paraphernalia, photos of dying soldiers and civilian massacres, and jars containing human fetuses, preserved in formaldehyde, that were deformed by exposure to defoliants.

Yun and I ride together on her Sirius, and Kanazawa

takes his own Super Cub. Since you don't need a license to
drive vehicles with motors up to 50 cc, most foreigners
buy bikes of that size and skip getting a license.

"Stop here, Hiro," Yun says, so I pull over in front of a
stand selling *nuoc mia*—sugar cane juice. Kanazawa stops
right behind us. *Nuoc mia* is an extremely popular drink in
this country. When you order, the vendor flips the switch
on his stalk-crusher machine and begins feeding sugar
cane through it to a considerable racket. You can't stand
too close, or you're likely to get splattered by flying juice.
Fresh squeezed *nuoc mia* is tasty but intensely sweet. It's
one of Yun's favorite drinks.

We all remain seated on our bikes as we wait. The vendor brings three small plastic bags, like the ones used to
take goldfish home from a shrine festival, and hands them
to Yun. She passes one forward to me, and one back to
Kanazawa. The bags are filled with the yellow juice and
tied tightly at the top with a rubber band around a little
straw. I lower my face mask so I can suck on the straw as I
pull back into traffic.

It's Sunday and the museum is jammed. A throng of
Westerners obviously belonging to a tour group clogs the
gate area. Yun gamely wades through the crowd and returns with tickets in hand. Once inside, we see plenty of
Vietnamese visitors as well.

Yun runs over to a heavy tank on display. Beckoning
with a big smile, she shouts, "Over here! Big tank!" She refuses to look at the deformed fetuses. "Very scary!" she
says with a shudder. Kanazawa studies the photographs

on exhibit one by one. In spite of what she said about being his guide, Yun has no information to offer about the individual photos, so she abandons that task and surveys the Western tourists in the crowd instead.

"That man look cool," she says.

The guy is wearing a T-shirt, walking shorts, and functional sandals. Over his shoulder is a backpack with a bottle of mineral water sticking out of its side pocket, and he has a Lonely Planet guidebook in his hand. His scaly white skin glows red with sunburn. No doubt he's American.

"I want to take picture."

"With him, you mean?"

"Yes. You ask, please, Hiro."

"Huh? Why me?"

"I am too shy. So please, you ask, yes?"

"Fine."

Feeling a little put upon, I walk up to the man and explain Yun's request. He readily consents. From up close I see that his face is covered in freckles. I suppose he has freckles all over his back, too. He strikes me as a what-you-see-is-what-you-get sort of guy. Probably a little younger than Yun.

"Say cheese!" I call out in English.

They stand with their backs to the tank and I snap the photo. Yun self-consciously offers her thanks and then comes running back. She looks happy.

"He is very nice."

"I was wondering, Yun," I say. "Doesn't it bother you about the war and the part Americans had in it?"

"Why? I not know the war."

I remember being a bit taken aback when I first arrived in Ho Chi Minh City. I'd come here assuming there'd be certain subjects like the war and the Communist Party that were too touchy to be discussed openly, so I was surprised to discover how completely loose everybody was about such things.

"And you actually like America, too."

"Yes. Vietnam young people, everybody like America, number-one best."

"But why?"

"America is big, and have many jobs, and easy to live. And people are very kind, too."

"Who told you that?"

"People who go there from here."

Have you ever considered they might just be painting a pretty picture?

"Many many people want to marry Americans," she adds.

"Is that what you want to do?"

"I not do. My mother hate Americans. Old people not like America. Young people, people who not know war, they like America."

In this country, the United States is still the ultimate symbol of wealth. Just as it was once upon a time for Japan. Japan was smitten with America after World War II.

American culture infected me, too. Vietnam may have won the war, but it has since been swallowed up by American culture. America's power is indeed mighty.

NOON IS APPROACHING. THE INTENSE HEAT HAS ALready parched our throats again. Yun and I buy some coconut water and find a bench in the shade where we can cool off as we quench our thirst. Since this is the dry season, it feels significantly cooler once we're out of direct sunlight. Like Kanazawa, I am making my second trip to the War Remnants Museum. I sit thinking about the last time I was here, when some of my students brought me right after I first arrived in Vietnam.

Yun droops limply on the bench beside me. Heat like this saps you of the desire to do anything at all.

After a while, Kanazawa reappears.

"I've had it. It's too hot," he says. "I just want to go home and take a nap."

"I'll second that."

"Me, too. I want to take nap."

"Shall we grab a little bite somewhere on the way, then?"

I turn to Yun. "What would you like to eat? Are you hungry?"

"Oh, yes. Very hungry."

"How about Bun Bo Hue?" I suggest. "In front of Co-op Mart."

"Yes. Let's go there."

While I'm waiting near the entrance for Yun and Kanazawa to retrieve the motorcycles from the parking lot, I see the guy who let us take his picture emerge from inside. He crosses the street and walks off in the direction of Reunification Palace. Motorcycle taxis looking for fares call after him one after the other, but he doesn't respond. Even in this heat, he's apparently determined to walk. He makes no effort to shield his pale skin, leaving it exposed without any defense against the searing rays of the sun.

I WAKE UP TO THE SOUND OF YUN'S VOICE, BUT SHE is not in bed beside me. I turn my head in the direction of her voice. She is huddled in the corner, talking into her cell phone.

I let out a yawn as I get to my feet. "What time is it?" I say before looking at my watch.

Stepping toward the balcony, I push open the French doors. A rush of fresh air and the din of the city wash over me.

An abundance of light pours into the room through the open windows. Blindingly intense. This is the land of light. The land of sunshine. In this place, fair skies are not called good weather. It is cloudy skies that get that seal of approval, for cloudless days are all but unbearable.

In the room behind me, Yun shouts angrily into her phone. Obviously, they're having another family argument. What could have set it off this time? She ends the call and lets out a howling *Arrgh!* before flopping down on the bed.

I sit down next to her. "A problem at home again?"

She stares mutely at the ceiling. She and her sisters are forever getting into disagreements about one thing or another, but like other families, the strength of the bond they share as a family remains beyond question. This seems to represent the continuing influence of Confucianism and is decidedly different from the way we Japanese perceive family today. I think in Japan we have the sense that we'd rather be with strangers we like than with family we don't, but such an attitude is unthinkable to Yun. The simple fact of being family trumps all other considerations in this culture, and since they also place great emphasis on respecting their elders, it's an exceptionally good place to be a parent.

Yun catches my eyes with a look that says *Hold me,* so I lie down next to her and begin gently stroking her head.

"So, tell me what happened."

"My sister yell at me again," she mumbles sullenly.

"For what?"

"Money. . . . I cannot pay back now. What money I have? I not have anything!"

Money again. Sometimes I think that's all this family ever talks about. Yun owes her sister a considerable sum. Hoping to pay off that debt, she started up a side export business to Korea two months ago, only to wind up getting cheated by someone on the Korean side and going even deeper into debt. But despite such misfortunes, Yun refuses to ask me to bail her out. It's a rare quality in a country where so many people descend on foreigners like flies on a feast.

"I sell things from work again," she says.

As a merchandise manager for an importer, she apparently knows how to doctor inventory numbers and redirect some of the goods when she gets particularly hard up for cash. It's a blatant crime, from my perspective, but in this country nobody seems to bat an eye when someone in accounting cooks the books and steals from the company, and people are constantly looking for ways to line their pockets. Enriching themselves is more important to them than enriching their company or their country. They don't realize that they're the ones who'll suffer in the end if the company's growth or the country's economic development falters.

"You know that's not right," I tell her.

"No worries, no worries. Everybody does it."

Isn't that what eventually makes the company go under?

AT LEAST TWICE A MONTH I GET CALLS FROM MY mother imploring me to come home. She won't give up.

Yun notices that I never phone her—she always phones me.

"Your mother worries for you," she scolds. "That's why she call you many times. Next time, you must call her."

No, I'm tempted to say, she's not worried the tiniest bit

about me. All she cares about is her own welfare, right there in Japan. But I doubt Yun would understand, so I just let it go. What I doubt she could ever understand are the feelings I have toward my mother. My entire relationship with my mother would be a mystery to her.

CHAPTER FIVE

AFTER WORK ON THURSDAY, I PULL UP in front of the department store where I'm supposed to meet Yun and sit astride my bike, waiting for her to arrive. This is the center of the city, so a substantial number of foreigners stand out among the pedestrians. Two young women from Japan looking every bit the tourists pass by within earshot. It feels refreshing to hear Japanese peppered with youthful slang for a change. You'd hardly guess it's the same language as the one I teach in my classes. Neither of the girls notices that I am Japanese. The drivers of motorcycle taxis and cyclos try to get their attention, and street vendors call out to them one after another. The people hustling for business in this part of town are all pretty sketchy.

"Hiro!"

By the time I hear my name and start to turn around, Yun is already pulling up beside me. She has a passenger on the back—a man I've never seen before.

"This is Takahashi-sensei," Yun says.

The man immediately jumps off the bike and repeats formally, "I'm Takahashi. Nice to meet you." I introduce myself to him.

"I invite Takahashi-sensei to eat with us," Yun tells me.

"All right, let's get to the restaurant first and then we can get acquainted. Where are we headed?"

"He never have *banh trang* Trang Bang, so we go there."

"You mean that place in District Three?"

"Yes."

She immediately scoots off again with Takahashi on the back, and I hurry after her, falling in close behind. It's not unusual for Yun to bring a friend or acquaintance along without saying anything beforehand, so I'm accustomed to that, but this is the first time she's shown up with a Japanese man in tow. I see her cheerfully chatting with him over her shoulder as she drives.

The restaurant's large dining room is nearly full. We are shown to an empty table in the corner. Yun hands Takahashi the menu. As he studies it, I study him. He's probably in his mid-twenties. He has a strong-willed brow, honest-looking eyes, and a kind mouth. His only immediately discernible flaw appears to be that he is short.

"I'll leave it to you," he says, handing the menu back to Yun.

"We want to order fish?" she asks, turning to me.

· "Yes, I think, since Takahashi-sensei is with us."

The large, whole steamed fish they serve here is way too much for two people. We probably won't be able to finish it all even with three of us sharing it.

"You like beer, Sensei?"

"No, I'll have a lime *soda chanh*."

"What you want, Hiro?"

"Coconut water."

"Okay. *Anh oi! Anh oi!*"

Yun calls a waiter over. As she orders, I ask Takahashi the question that always comes first when you meet someone new from Japan in Ho Chi Minh City.

"How long have you been here?"

"About six months. How about you?"

"It's been two years for me. Do you plan to stay long?"

"No, only a year."

When the waiter is done taking our order, Yun turns to me. "Takahashi-sensei come from Tokyo," she announces with a bright smile.

"Oh, I'm from Tokyo, too," I say. "This is a surprise. I almost never run into fellow Tokyoites overseas."

"Well, strictly speaking, I'm from Saitama. But I tell my students Tokyo because they wouldn't have any idea where that is. I figure everybody knows Tokyo, so that's close enough."

"Sensei, next week, you can teach us song, please?"

"A song?" he says. "What song?"

"'Blue Rabbit' by Noriko Sakai. We want to sing."

Several years ago a television series from Japan starring

the singer and actress Noriko Sakai aired on Vietnamese TV. Its theme song, "Blue Rabbit," caught on in a big way. Even years later, she remains extremely popular, and students of Japanese invariably ask you to teach them the song. I managed to get hold of a tape after arriving in Vietnam, and I teach the song to nearly all of my classes.

"You already know that song, Yun. You even have it on tape."

"But it's very difficult, and I still cannot sing. Other students want to learn, too, they say."

"All right. I'm not sure we can fit it in next week, but we can plan to do it sometime."

"Yes, then everybody very happy," Yun says, beaming. The Vietnamese really love to sing.

The waiter brings us a basket tray piled high with lettuce, perilla, mint, and other aromatic herbs and greens, along with platters of boiled pork, steamed fish, and rice-paper wrappers.

"Wow, it's huge!" Takahashi turns wide-eyed at the sight of the fish.

"Yes, you must eat big," Yun urges him. "Put food you like in wrapper."

"Do I put the fish in, too?" he asks as he places greens on a wrapper.

"Yes, put the fish in. It is very good. Eating only the fish is okay, too."

He stuffs his first wrapper a little too full. As he takes a bite, pieces of fish and torn greens fall from the loosely rolled rice paper onto his plate.

Yun laughs. "You put in too much," she says. Takahashi laughs, too.

Rows of fluorescent tubes glare down from the ceiling. The intense illumination lights up every bit of litter scattered across the floor, from torn greens and fish bones to dirty paper napkins and cigarette butts. A large ceiling fan rotates overhead, right in the middle of the room.

"Sensei, you go to Bin Quoi yet?" Yun asks.

"Bin Quoi? Where is that?"

"At Thanh Da."

"Thanh Da?"

"It's a town inside a big circular curve in the Saigon River about thirty minutes from here," I explain. "Though it's actually more country than town."

"No, I've never been there."

"This Sunday, let's go there," says Yun. "It's very beautiful place."

"There's a resort there called Bin Quoi Tourist Village where they have a huge outdoor buffet every weekend. You'll be impressed," I tell him.

A travel agency owns and operates the resort. It's true that it's beautiful, but it has a distinctly man-made quality about it, too. I sometimes take daytime rides out to the larger area known as Thanh Da, where the tourist village is located. I can turn off onto an unpaved side road and in no time at all find myself in the middle of rice paddies stretching into the distance all around me, negotiating a path barely wide enough for a single bike atop the divider between paddies. I'll hear ducks quacking and see them swimming about in the water.

"Can we ask some other teachers to come along, too?" he asks.

"Yes, let's go everybody together."

"Can we get there by bicycle?"

"Not bicycle. But no worries. I ask other students, so teachers can ride on motorcycles. On back."

"You don't drive a motorcycle?" I ask.

"The school won't let us. They say it's too dangerous."

"Just for Japanese, I suppose?"

"Yes."

"It's too bad," Yun says. "You should see Hiro. She drive faster than us."

"Wow. And you've never gotten hurt?"

"I've had one accident. Though not serious."

"I have accident three times," Yun says.

"So people do have accidents. I guess when you look at what it's like out there, it'd be ridiculous to think otherwise."

"But you're actually worse off on a bicycle, you know. In a collision between a bicycle and a motorcycle, the motorcycle's always going to win."

"I suppose so, since we share the same roads. And we even travel at pretty much the same speed."

"Yun, could you ask for some more greens?"

"It seems like all you've been eating is greens," Takahashi says.

"Hiro like vegetables very much."

"I'm basically an herbivore," I say.

Yun gets the waiter's attention and he soon plops a fresh pile of greens on our table.

Yun and Takahashi talk mostly about the other teachers and students at their school. He seems like the serious, conscientious sort. Even when she's excitedly bubbling on and on about something, he always maintains a certain teacherly gravitas in the way he responds to her.

AS I'D ANTICIPATED, WE FAIL TO FINISH OFF ALL OF the fish in spite of Takahashi's valiant contribution to the effort.

After driving a short distance from the restaurant together, Yun turns off to the right to take her teacher home. I ride on by myself along Cach Mang Thang Tam Street, which is still bustling. Even at this late hour, traffic is surprisingly heavy, and I soon find it annoying enough that I decide to escape onto a side street. As I drive along the narrow street, I can see right into most of the houses that crowd both sides. Because it's so hot here all year round, people don't generally close their windows while they're still up and about, relying on the sturdy steel bars that cover the openings to guard against the high incidence of burglaries. Suddenly I start to feel anxious, and hurry toward home.

Not far from where I live, I pass through an area where streetwalkers look for customers. I spot a number of them on the job tonight, too. They're all so pretty, and young, yet they have to sell their bodies for the equivalent of just four hundred yen.

Back in my room I discover a parade of ants marching across the floor and I'm annoyed all over again. The slightest lapse in vigilance and this is what you get. If you leave anything sweet lying around, they sniff it out in no time. So the rule is that all food items either go in the refrigerator or get hung on the clothesline strung across the room. Even then, the little buggers are likely to find their way along the rope. These southern ants are a determined bunch.

This time their prize is a half-eaten sweet roll left on the table. Yun's. I scoop the ant-covered pastry into a plastic grocery bag and close the top of the bag around the spray tip of some bug killer, bunching it tightly around the nozzle so the ants have no escape. Then I press the button. It's a powerful insecticide, and the ants die quickly. I tie the bag securely shut and drop it in the trash before directing my spray at the ants still wandering about the room. In an amusingly short time they are all dead, and I quickly sweep their carcasses out onto the balcony with a broom. Finally I can sit down and catch my breath. Yun's still not back. The staff housing where Takahashi lives is only about five minutes away by motorcycle. She should be home by now if all she's doing is dropping him off.

Collecting myself, I turn to preparations for tomorrow's classes. On my agenda are several handouts, which I begin tapping out on my computer. Before long I am completely absorbed in my work.

As I finish up, I glance at my watch. Almost midnight. It's late. Did she have an accident? Or get hit by a bag snatcher? It's dangerous to be out alone after eleven.

I send off a text message but get no reply. I try calling, too, but she doesn't answer. Unfortunately, I never got Takahashi's number. I'm becoming crazy with worry, but at a loss what else to do, I just keep calling her number over and over.

About one o'clock, I finally get a text message: "I not come home tonight. Good night."

"Why? What happened?" I text back immediately. She does not reply.

I get into bed but find it impossible to sleep. I search for Yun's scent on the sheets and pillows.

When we spend all our time together, I occasionally find myself wanting a few moments to myself, but for nearly two years now, being with her has become as natural a part of my day as eating meals, and to suddenly have her missing from beside me is like being deprived of oxygen and having to gasp for breath. It's only with the warmth of her body and the smell of her skin beside me that I can fall peacefully asleep.

A feeling of foreboding comes over me. It sets my mind racing. I toss and turn endlessly.

I finally drift off into a shallow sleep about the time the sky is beginning to grow light, and I greet the morning a very long way from refreshed.

. . . .

THE NEXT DAY, I BEGIN TEXTING AND CALLING YUN
as soon as I'm awake. She ignores me. There have been
times in the past when we had a fight and didn't see each
other for a day or so, but unless my memory utterly fails
me, nothing like that has occurred this time.

What could this be about? The only possible explanation I can think of is . . . Takahashi?

Sometimes I simply lose all sense of what is going on
inside Yun's head.

The demands of work keep me occupied during the
day, but when I return home in the evening and have a
chance to catch my breath, my chest begins to constrict
with that feeling of foreboding again. Being here all by
myself unsettles me. The room is much too quiet without
Yun, which makes me feel all the more bereft.

I walk out onto the balcony and look down over the
railing. A dog is scampering by below. It's hard to tell
whether it could be someone's pet or if it's just a stray.

The Vietnamese flag lashed to the railing of an apartment across the road is at rest in the absence of any wind,
a spiritless streak of red in the deep purple darkness.

I hear the buzz of motorcycles and the barking of
dogs.

Even at this midnight hour, the clouds overhead are
eerily lit up, tinted a pinkish hue. It reminds me of the
bright, starless sky over Tokyo, and I gaze up at it without
expectation, just as I used to do back home. Too many
things get in the way for me to see it as it really is. The flat,
featureless sky tells me nothing.

. . .

FOR A SECOND FULL DAY, I FAIL TO REACH YUN. SHE has never shut me out for this long before.

What did I do?

Or is it something I didn't do?

THEN AT 8:23 ON SUNDAY MORNING, A TEXT MESSAGE comes. I am still asleep in bed when the goofy little tone announcing its arrival awakens me. I reach for my phone on the night table.

Seeing that it's from Yun, I'm immediately wide awake. I open the message:

"I not see you again. Goodbye."

For the longest time, all I can do is stare at the words.

Minutes go by, and finally my mental faculties return to me.

Huh?

What're you saying?

How . . . ?

Why . . . ?

What happened . . . ?

To bring this on . . . ?

What is she trying to say?

What can she be thinking?

I can't make heads or tails of it.

I try calling again, and this time her phone is turned on. She answers on the fifth ring.

"Why? I don't understand at all! Goodbye? What for? How can you ignore my calls and messages for two whole days? And then suddenly it's you won't see me anymore, goodbye? What is this? What's going on?"

I'm so upset that the words come rushing out in a single breath.

"You are angry now," she says, "so I not talk to you." It's impossible to read the tone of her voice over the phone.

"But you—"

"I hang up now."

"Now just one minute!" I can't keep my rising anger from showing.

"You like Konno-san, yes?"

"Huh?"

"So I think about that. After all, it's best to be with man. I am same like everybody—I want to get married. My mother, she want me to hurry up get married, too. Takahashi-sensei is good man. And Konno-san, he make good boyfriend for you."

"W-wait a second—"

"Thank you, Hiro. For many, many things."

"But even if you want to be with Takahashi-sensei, we can still be friends, can't we?"

"No."

"Why not?"

"It's strange, Hiro."

"It is not!" My voice rises again.

"I give you best wishes for your work. I must go now."

"Wait, Yun!"

I hear an infuriating click and then she's gone. I hurry to call her back, but she has already turned off her phone.

I can't sort out the jumble of thoughts in my head. Could what we had really be over, just like that? What happened to the deep bond I felt between us? Was that only me? And everything that I thought we'd built together—was it only a figment of my imagination?

"How can you do this to me, Yun? You idiot!"

My stomach twists into a throbbing knot and I double over in pain.

Even with the curtains pulled tight, I can feel the sun beating down beyond them. It wearies me to imagine how hot it must already be outside.

I lie in bed unable to move, enduring the pain. A cacophony of thoughts spins round and round in my head.

First, there was Yun and me.

And then . . .

Me and Konno.

And therefore . . .

Yun and Takahashi?

Which means?

Which means?

Which means?

I try desperately to fit the pieces together, but cannot shape them into a coherent whole. The circuits in my brain keep replaying the same strains over and over, like a broken CD player.

Remembering I have a bottle of banana liquor that

Kanazawa gave me some time ago, I dig it out from the back of the cupboard and take a swig. It's strong stuff. I can barely tolerate the taste, but nevertheless swallow several more gulps, hoping that it might calm my runaway emotions.

A warm sensation slowly spreads through my body, then all of a sudden I break into chills. My stomach heaves and I rush into the bathroom. Since I've had nothing to eat, digestive juices are all that come up. My stomach remains gripped with nausea.

I collapse onto the bed and press my eyes shut.

"Ugghh, I feel so sick. Please, Yun, come take care of me. Bring me some water."

Tears spill from my eyes. What am I ever going to do with myself on a Sunday without Yun?

"Oh, I miss you so much, Yun! Why are you doing this to me? You stupid idiot!"

I sorely wish now that I'd left the liquor alone, but it's too late for such regrets. The bottle that was supposed to ease my pain has only compounded my misery. All I can do is lie there in tears, talking to myself on and on. In time, the nausea finally subsides—only to be replaced by a searing headache.

"Oh, come on! Give me a break!" I cry out.

Rummaging through my desk drawer, I find what's left of the pain pills we bought when Yun had her hemorrhoid surgery. Take two, it says. The thought of washing down all six remaining pills flashes through my mind, but I think better of it and swallow the prescribed two.

A short while later, an irresistible drowsiness comes over me as I lie weeping, and before I know it, I have drifted off to sleep.

IT IS NEARLY EVENING BY THE TIME I AWAKE. THE headache has disappeared, but I remain an emotional wreck. If something doesn't change this before nightfall, I'm afraid things will go from bad to worse.

I step out onto the balcony and look down toward Hai's café. The usual group of men is there, reading their newspapers or staring off into space.

Overhead, a slight tinge is coming into the sky, coloring the mackerel clouds in a gradient of pale orange light. During the wet season, we often get rain at this time of day, but this is the dry season, so we rarely see any precipitation.

I decide I need a change of scenery. After a quick shower, I head out into the gathering dusk on my motorcycle. I ride aimlessly about town, round and round.

On one of the main thoroughfares, a luxury car carrying what appears to be a Japanese businessman pulls past me in traffic. Watching the man's head through the rear window as the car recedes into the distance, I think of Konno.

He remains on my mind while I continue driving about. After three more circuits around the city center, I take out my phone and call him.

. . .

WHEN I GET TO HIS OFFICE, KONNO IS, AS USUAL, toiling alone.

"Working all by yourself on a Sunday again," I say. "You poor thing."

"Oh, give it a rest. I'm just about ready to quit, so why don't you have a seat there while you wait."

He motions me to the usual chair. As I watch Konno working, looking and acting the same as ever, something that's been wound up inside me gradually begins to loosen. I'm saved, I think to myself, and desperately blink back the tears that are once more welling in my eyes.

"Well, I guess that's enough for today. There's basically no end to it. I'll pick up here tomorrow. Sorry to keep you waiting. So, what would you like to eat?"

He comes over to me, right next to where I'm sitting. I stand and look into his eyes.

"How about Italian?" he says.

I pause. "Sounds great, but . . . first," I say and wrap my arms around him.

"Huh? What's this about? What's going on?"

His flustered tone warms my heart.

"Please. Just let me stay like this for a minute. I'm sorry, but, please, let me just stay like this."

His broad chest. His smell. The scent of a man. A scent that sets my heart hammering, and yet is so reassuring.

Though a little haltingly at first, Konno begins gently stroking my hair. I cannot stop a flood of tears.

"Did something painful happen?"

I break into convulsive sobs and he folds me tightly

into his big, strong arms. Holding me like that without saying a word, he waits patiently for me to regain my composure.

"I'm sorry. I'll be okay now. I think. Probably. I really am so sorry. Barging in like this when you're busy with work."

"Well, at any rate, let's start by getting something to eat. How does that sound?"

He takes me to an Italian restaurant known for serving some of the best food in town. It's the first pizza and pasta I've eaten in quite some time, and by asking no questions, Konno makes it possible for me to simply enjoy the food. I'm grateful for his consideration.

"Do you ever wish you could go home to Japan?" I ask.

"You bet."

"Today, for the first time since coming here, I really wished I could go home."

"I think wanting to go home is normal when you're living somewhere else. You haven't been back for something like two years, right?"

"Uh-huh. But somehow, I don't know, I feel disappointed in myself for being so weak."

"You know, this is something I've been wondering from before, but why are you so determined to be totally self-reliant? As a woman, what would be wrong with getting married, or at least letting yourself be more dependent on a man?"

"If I got married, I'd probably just get divorced."

"Why should you assume that even before you start?

There're more couples who don't get divorced than who do, you know."

"Because the divorce rate in my family is so high."

"It's really that bad?"

"Over eighty percent."

"*Ai-yi-yi*. Well, in that case, maybe you're out of luck."

"You think? Anyway, I've accepted it. It's just that . . ." I stop, searching for the right words.

"Yeah?" he says gently, prodding me to continue.

"I'm human, too, so I have moments of weakness sometimes."

After I say it, he takes a drink of his red wine and his eyes drift to a spot a little above my head.

"And this is one of those times?"

"I think so."

"Is there something I can do to help?" he asks, now looking me straight in the eye.

"Maybe."

KONNO IS VERY GENTLE. HE IS GENTLE, AND YET A man's caresses are rougher than a woman's. I'm aroused not just by his touch, but by the strength of it. I feel my body responding in ways I can scarcely believe, and I'm embarrassed when I'm unable to keep from crying out. His strength, his masculinity transport me. Over and over, he pulls back from the brink, until I can no longer bear it. I beg him to finish.

My vagina quivers. Tiny twitches ripple through me even after his penis is gone.

Lying in Konno's arms, I revel in a moment of repose. Body heat and heartbeats bring us a sense of security. I kiss his nipple. The hair on his chest tickles my nose. It's such a cute little nipple, but I can't help finding it wanting. I yearn for Yun's breasts, and feel a wave of sadness.

Near dawn, I slip quietly out of bed and steal from the apartment, taking care not to wake Konno.

Mornings during the dry season bring a chill. The faster I go, the wider awake I become.

I feel worlds better than I did yesterday. It fills me with exhilaration.

As I savor the feeling of disturbance lingering inside my softest place, I look up at the changing colors of the dawning sky.

THE BOSS FLEW TO JAPAN ON BUSINESS OVER THE weekend, so we have no Monday meeting. More than a few of the instructors failed to get the word ahead of time and trickle in at the usual hour. When they learn that the meeting has been canceled, everyone except those who have morning classes at the center promptly departs again.

My first order of business is to prepare for my afternoon classes, but I have difficulty concentrating. Before long, I catch myself replaying the sensation of Konno's penis inside me last night. I was so incredibly turned on, and no man had ever lifted me so quickly to a climax before. Had completion with a man always felt so good? I can only think that my body's sensitivity must have been heightened by the sensual abandon Yun and I enjoyed for so long.

I drift off into a world of fantasy, thinking how much I want to do it with Konno again, if the opportunity should arise.

"Azuma-sensei? Azuma-sensei?"

The sound of someone calling my name bursts through my daydream, pulling me back to reality. I look up to see who it is, and my eyes meet Ito's. His desk is directly opposite mine. He's been busy making a drawing on an oversized sheet of paper.

"Yes? What is it?"

"Do you have any wide-tip markers? Something besides red and black?"

"Let me see, I've got blue and green, and, oh, I've got orange, too. Here."

"Thanks. I forgot my set at home today."

"What unit are you making that drawing for?"

"Verbs of existence."

"You've done a great job. You're talented."

I stand and walk around beside his desk for a better look. The drawing shows the inside of a room. In the middle of the room is a round table, and on the table are some apples and oranges and bananas. On the right wall is a door, in front of which stands a young boy. In the back corner, on the left, is a desk with several books, ballpoint pens, and notebooks strewn carelessly across the top. A cat lies beneath the desk, and next to it is a large window with a view of the scene outside: a young girl playing with her dog. The various elements will let him drill sentences like "What is on the table?" "Where is the cat?" "The boy is in front of the door," "The dictionary is on the desk," and so on, so that students can learn proper use of the animate and inanimate verbs of existence.

"Actually, I used to do manga, once upon a time. I really enjoy drawing."

"Have you been making other visual aids like this?"

"Sure, a bunch of them. I have so much fun doing them, sometimes it's morning before I realize it."

"Could I see them?"

"Oh, yeah, sure. I keep them right in here. If you see anything you think you can use, just help yourself."

He opens his bottom desk drawer, which is organized by lesson with everything neatly labeled.

"Wow! Look how organized you are. You're a type-A personality, I bet."

"Well, my room's a mess."

"Looks like you really went all out on this one," I say, holding up a drawing from the drawer. "It's to practice making requests, right?"

"It gives me a big sense of satisfaction when I'm making stuff like this. Figuring out, through trial and error, exactly how I can most effectively get the lesson across to the students is probably my favorite part of teaching."

"You mean, even more than the classes?"

"Well, I enjoy the classes, too—especially when my students are surprised or amused or ask questions right where I intended. But an awful lot of the time they don't react the way I expect, and I haven't learned to appreciate that yet."

"Right. Things never do go exactly according to plan, do they?"

"Still, it's highly satisfying work—except for the low pay."

"Then maybe you should start your own school?"

"You know, I'm actually thinking of something along those lines—if I decide to keep teaching," he says, sounding as though nothing could make him happier.

THAT EVENING, I'M STILL AT THE OFFICE WORKING on lesson plans for the next day when Konno calls. I love that moment of nervous anticipation before I press the TALK button.

"Hello."

"It's Konno. Are you doing okay?" he asks with concern. "Did you work today?"

I feel my entire body responding to the sound of his voice—from its memory of last night.

"I'm at work now. And yes, I'm fine. I should apologize. I left without saying anything."

"No, no, never mind that. But . . ."

"Yes?"

"Would you like to have dinner again tonight?"

"All right. I'll come by in a little bit."

Yamada is the only other person still at the office, and she pounces with curiosity the moment I click off.

"Who was that? A guy? Come on, tell me. A new boyfriend?"

"Hmm . . ." I grunt ambiguously.

I don't really know the answer myself. But I do know that my vagina is already licking its lips and drooling in anticipation. It's just itching for the chance to swallow him up again tonight.

AS I WAIT FOR KONNO IN BED AFTER TAKING MY shower first, my mind wanders to Yun. Would it sadden her to know that I've slept with Konno?

He comes to me with his hair still dripping and plants a kiss on my forehead. Our eyes meet, and we hold each other's gaze for a moment. Every so often, I see a peculiar light come into his eyes, but I have yet to learn what it means. Slowly lowering his gaze, he takes my nipple in his mouth. To watch someone sucking on my nipple is a curious sensation. Even as I experience sexual pleasure, I feel as though I've become that person's mother. The grandest of men is like a baby to me when I see him sucking at my breast; in my eyes, he's a creature much weaker than me.

Since he asks me to, I take Konno's penis in my mouth. Fellatio hurts my jaw. The up-and-down motion strains my neck. And sometimes I nearly choke when I'm hit in the back of the throat. So I'm already thinking how much better I like cunnilingus, when I glance up and see the smugness on Konno's face. He looks utterly detached, as if he could be perusing the Compendium of Laws while I'm sucking him off. My blood rises, and I purposely pump harder with my mouth. He grimaces and pulls away. Fending off his attempt to roll on top of me, I climb astride him and move my hips up and down. Climax comes almost right away, and then my whole body goes limp. His own climax incomplete, Konno promptly turns me under him and begins thrusting up into me.

Why am I responding so intensely? It feels so impossibly good, I think I'm just going to melt away, head and genitals and all.

IF I HAD A PENIS, I'D WANT TO TRY IT OUT ON YUN. I'd want to take her from on top and on bottom, and from in front and behind.

Which in no way means that I wish I were a man. I merely wish I could have a penis as a woman, and could bury it between another woman's legs to experience the sensation of the vagina through my penis. And also to see that woman lifted on my shaft into throes of blissful ecstasy.

CHAPTER SIX

WITH A SUDDEN CRAVING FOR THE junky flavor of fast food, I make a noon-hour run to Lotteria. The cost for just a cheeseburger and fries with a drink is nearly four times what I pay for a Vietnamese lunch. As I sit munching on my burger, a man with the prominent features of a Korean takes the next table over. I notice him glancing my way from time to time. Neither the burger nor the fries are as good here as at Lotteria in Japan. The man's continuing glances finally make me look his way, and our eyes meet, which he promptly takes as his opportunity to strike up a conversation.

"You're Japanese, aren't you?" he says in English with a smile.

He looks a bit like the Korean actor Song Kang-ho. A chunky man, big-boned and muscular—which is a body

type common among Koreans, but not seen among Vietnamese. His physique plainly marks him as a foreigner, so
he's no doubt popular with women, but also an easy target for scammers. I'd put him at about my own age.

"Do you live here?" he goes on.

I don't think I've ever met a Korean man who's so
forward.

"Yes."

Of all the Korean actors I've seen, Song Kang-ho is my
favorite.

"A student?"

"I work."

"What do you do?"

"I teach Japanese."

"Do you enjoy it?"

"Yes, it's a lot of fun. How about you? What do you
do?"

"I work for Samsung. Though I'm a local hire, so they
don't pay me very well. Until a year ago, I was working in
Canada."

"You came from Canada to Vietnam?"

"Yes. And I was in America before that."

"Do you plan to stay in Vietnam long?"

"Probably not. It's not such a great place."

"So you'll go back to Korea?"

"Hardly."

"Why not?"

"It'd just be a drag. I'll move on to some other country
and find a job."

A person who shares my scent. I feel as if I'm looking into a mirror. He sniffed me out.

It might not be so bad to spend my life drifting about the world with a man like this. In fact, could it be that's exactly the kind of life I'm really looking for?

I can't help thinking that people like us, who can't stay put at home, must be missing something that other people have; and in its place, we must have something else that they lack.

A FULL WEEK HAS GONE BY SINCE I LAST SAW YUN. It's the first time since I came to Vietnam that I've been without her for this long. We met the day after my arrival, and from then until now, we saw each other nearly every day. My life in Ho Chi Minh City has depended on her in so many ways that not having her around leaves a huge hole.

I've been sending her messages and trying to reach her on the phone every day, but she refuses to respond. With each additional day of rejection, with each new morning that I awaken to find her still missing, I sense the strength of her resolve.

I long to see her, for a chance to talk it all through. At this point it's really only to sort out my own feelings and come to some kind of closure, but since Yun seems not to want it, I need to simply move on. If I love her, I have to let her follow her own heart. If she wants to leave me, I have to let her go.

I FIND THE STUDENTS IN MY TRAINEE CLASS BUB-
bling with excitement.

"Sensei, they tell us, day we go Japan!"

"When will it be?"

"The fortieth of next month."

"The fourteenth."

"Oh, yes, the fourteenth."

"That's great news! You must all be happy."

"Yes!"

Everyone is beaming.

"Where will you work in Japan?" I ask the class leader,
Long.

"Me and Nhan-san, Khai-san, Minh-san, we go Shizu-
oka. Quyet-san, Nam-san, Chinh-san, they go Osaka.
Hue-san, Son-san, Duc-san, they go Gunma. Others not
know."

Which means five of them have yet to be placed. After
completing their language training, my students sometimes get left hanging for as much as six months before a
company can be found to sponsor them. When that happens, they join another class and continue studying until
their placements come through. I'm a little surprised that
Minh is among those who found a spot right away.

So, how many of these men are planning to bolt, I
wonder.

Back in the office, Yamada is sitting with her elbows on

her desk, glaring at the timetable for native Japanese instructors.

"Why the look?" I ask.

"We have a problem, Hiro."

"What is it this time?"

"Miyahara's done it again."

"When it comes to that woman, there's not much that would surprise me anymore."

Miyahara is . . . well . . . a social misfit. Both back at home in Japan and here in Vietnam. She's officially one of the full-timers at the center, but it remains a mystery why she was ever hired. The most likely theory says that her father is some kind of big shot in Japanese government or financial circles, and as an acquaintance, the boss simply could not say no. Judging from the way she throws money around, I have little doubt that she had a pampered upbringing. She buys a thousand-dollar motorcycle without batting an eye, and when it gets stolen three days later, she promptly goes out and buys another. She's ditzy and easily distracted, which makes her an easy target, so she keeps losing her wallet or bag to thieves, but she hardly seems to mind. At thirty-one years old, she behaves more like a child. It's not unusual for her to forget that she has a class to teach and go off on a jaunt somewhere, or simply sleep in late. Even the Vietnamese instructors are appalled by her lack of responsibility, but her father's powerful position apparently makes it impossible for the boss to fire her. The ones who suffer most are the students.

"She didn't show for her class this morning, so I thought maybe she'd overslept again and figured I just needed to go wake her up."

Although Yamada, Hayashi, and I live farther away, most of the Japanese on staff are housed in the employee residence next door to the center, so it's easy to go knock on their doors.

"I suppose you found her chomping on rice crackers and watching TV?"

"Nope. It turns out she went back to Japan. On the red-eye last night."

"Japan? You're kidding? Nobody had said anything, right?"

"Nope. But I guess the boss got a call from her father this morning."

"That's typical. So, is she coming back?"

"The word is that she's going to take a little bit of a break in Japan, and then she'll return."

"What happens to her classes?"

"The rest of us'll have to fill in, obviously."

"Oh, come on! How can she do this to us? What do we need her for? Will somebody please just fire her!"

"The boss is at his wits' end, too. Anyway, I need to talk to you. At the moment, you're open in the evening on Monday, Thursday, and Saturday, and in the early-morning slot, every day but Tuesday, right?"

"I don't like the sound of this."

"Can I ask you to cover her classes on Monday and Thursday evening, and Wednesday and Friday morning?"

"So evening and morning both? Ouch. Well, I guess there's really no choice. Fine, I'll take them."

"You're a lifesaver. I think maybe that should get us through."

"Any idea when our wayward princess might be coming back?"

"I'm told next week or the week after."

I groan. "It must be nice to be her. Mind if I make a straw doll and put a hex on her?"

"Let me drive a nail through it, too."

Miyahara may come from a good family, but you'd never guess it from her appearance. She's badly out of shape, has a double chin, wears an ugly perm that makes her look fifty, and she smells. In a word, she's a complete slob. Half-empty glasses of juice and forgotten pieces of fruit sit around her room rotting and wafting foul odors into the air, and since she also leaves her windows wide open, cockroaches and rats and ants come and go as they please. Her clothes are heaped in piles everywhere, and she wears sweat-stained outfits that make you wonder when they were last laundered.

The staff residence is a three-story house with a full kitchen and living room on the first floor, and three bedrooms each on the second and third, so it can accommodate up to six people. It used to be that the second floor was the men's floor, with just Ito and Mikami, while the three women occupied the third floor. But Kishimoto, in the middle room, got fed up with the odors and pests that came her way from Miyahara's side and moved down to the second floor. That leaves Miyahara sharing the floor with Murai, who seems to find her floormate's habits a considerable annoyance even with an empty room as a buffer between them.

"By the way," Yamada says, changing the subject, "does Yun have a Japanese boyfriend now?"

My heart almost pops out of my chest at this unexpected query.

"Who told you that?"

"I saw her myself," she says. "Yesterday. Riding her motorcycle with a guy. Acting like a couple of love birds. There's no other way to describe it."

I can feel the blood rushing to my head.

"He's a Japanese teacher. I met him once," I say.

"He teaches at her school?"

"Uh-huh. But you have to wonder about his taste, don't you? There's lots of prettier girls around."

"He could do a whole lot worse than to have Yun looking after him. It should be interesting."

"But she's really not the kind of girl that men go for."

"What're you being so negative about? I suppose you're feeling lonely now that Yun has a boyfriend all of sudden."

"Don't be silly."

"You know what I think, Hiro? I think you got to be too dependent on Yun. You need to try standing on your own two feet for a change."

Her words hit me like a thunderbolt. So that's the pic-

ture people have of me? That I don't stand on my own
two feet?

AT LUNCHTIME, THE ENTIRE JAPANESE STAFF, MINUS
Miyahara and Hayashi, go to a café that's well known
among the local residents in town. We're shown to a table
on the terrace, facing the street. The place looks very
trendy from the outside, but the menu is standard Vietnamese fare. We order grilled chicken thighs, boiled fish,
sautéed water spinach, a mushroom-tofu stir-fry, and for
soup, a sweet-sour *canh chua* with tomato and vegetables
and beef. All are staple menu items.

Vietnamese cuisine uses great quantities of vegetables.
When freshly picked, the vegetables remain crisp and aromatic even after cooking; the flavors are rich and have a
certain sweetness. For chicken they use free-range local
birds rather than mass-produced broilers, and they
butcher and cook them on the same day so they are as
fresh as they could possibly be. The meat is firm and juicy,
the flavor full-bodied and sweet.

The vast majority of dishes are very healthy, and I suppose that's why most Vietnamese are so slim. But they
routinely eat two and three bowls of rice with their
meals. Some people even consume four meals a day—and
still they remain thin. Most women have exceptionally
slender figures, and next to them, Japanese women of average height and weight come out looking quite robust.

Our bone structure is simply that much larger. Most of the Vietnamese women in my own circles are quite thin, too. They say being skinny makes you look poor, so they'd like to put on more weight, but they simply can't, no matter how much they eat. On the other hand, with the growth of the affluent classes in recent years, the country does seem to be seeing an increase in obesity, especially among children.

The food arrives on large platters. We each serve ourselves from these communal dishes, taking just as much as we want. The rice is mounded in a container that looks like a washbasin; the soup comes in a vessel the size of a mixing bowl, filled to the brim.

"Have you decided what you'll have your trainees do for their speaking test next week?" Yamada asks Ito as we all start eating.

I'm sitting with Mikami on my right and Yamada to my left. Ito is across the table from Yamada, and with him on that side are Kishimoto and then Murai.

Ito looks up from the chicken thigh he holds between his hands as he chews. "Yes," he says. "All I did was make a few adjustments to the format you've used before."

"So Q and A and self-introductions?"

"I'll also have them read some numbers and make some sentences."

"Make some sentences?"

"I give the student a word, and he has to make a sentence that contains it."

"For instance?"

"Like I say 'bananas,' and the student might say 'I will go to the market to buy some bananas.'"

"Or he might just play it safe with something easy like, 'Bananas are delicious.'"

The other three at the table seem to be too busy eating to pay attention to this conversation. Murai in particular is completely absorbed in removing the bones from her fish.

"So do you think I need to say what grammatical pattern the student has to use, too?"

"That might do it. What do you think, Hiro?"

"Yes, I think you do need to specify a pattern. Then, so long as you choose the right words to give them, it should work fine."

"Uh-huh. Be sure to consider your choice of words carefully," Yamada agrees.

"All right."

Having finished his piece of chicken, Ito starts in on his water spinach, alternating with large mouthfuls of rice. Soon he goes for a second helping of rice.

"It looks like you're doing okay with Vietnamese food now," I say as I watch him filling his bowl from the big rice basin.

"Yes. My palate has finally adapted to the seasonings they use," he replies happily, a thin film of perspiration glistening on his forehead.

"If you don't hurry up and eat, your food's going to get

cold," I say to Yamada, who looks like she's more interested in continuing the conversation. She has not yet
touched anything on her plate.

"Right. Time to eat," she says, and finally picks up her
chopsticks.

"I was wondering," Mikami says, looking at Yamada.
"Is that Tam woman going to be joining our staff?"

"Tam?" Kishimoto says, a question in her voice.

"She came to the office with the boss a couple of days
ago. Her Japanese is really good, and she's cute, too."

"I missed that. I never saw her," she says, and then
turns to Murai next to her. "Did you know about her?"

"Not at all," she says, shaking her head. She is still
pulling bones out of her fish.

"I guess she was working in Japan until just last
month."

This Vietnamese woman named Tam appears to have
caught Mikami's eye.

By my guess, Mikami is around fifty years old. Although he refuses to go into the details, before coming to
Vietnam he lived in Italy for a while, where a venture he
was part of went belly up, and that somehow led to him
coming here. Since all that we know about his time in
Italy came directly from him, there's really no way for
anyone to verify his story. The man is always looking for a
good time, but he's also unbelievably cheap. He acts as if
it's only natural for his students to pick up the tab for him.
Meanwhile, the students treat him with great respect because he's their elder and their teacher—not to mention

from Japan. But his taste is decidedly vulgar: for example, he's a frequent visitor to the touchy-feely bars known as *bia om*. While he shows little inclination to cooperate with his colleagues on anything, he fawns endlessly on the boss. He often seems to be doing something secretive on the side, and it's patently obvious that he's trying his best to avoid Yamada and me—which, to me, makes him highly suspicious. For all any of us knows, he could be using his teaching job as cover for trafficking in humans or something. Especially when you consider how lousy his teaching is. You can tell his heart isn't in it at all.

"Yes, as a trainee," Yamada confirms.

Kishimoto is struggling mightily to pick up a small, slippery mushroom in the stir-fry with her chopsticks.

"I wonder if it was hard for her," I say.

"It seems like a lot of the people here who can speak Japanese did stints in Japan as trainees," Murai says with a look of satisfaction at having finally finished her fish.

"I understand she was only getting thirty thousand yen a month," Mikami says, then holds his bowl out to me. "Could I get a refill of rice?" The basin is at the far end of the table, diagonally in front of Ito, so I pass the bowl across to him. While he's at it, I quickly shovel in my last two bites and hand him my own bowl as well.

"Thirty thousand a month?" Ito says with rounded eyes, as he takes my bowl.

"I imagine they deducted her rent and utilities off the top, and the rest went automatically into some kind of compulsory savings account," Yamada says. She finishes the last of her soup and holds her bowl out to me. "Seconds, please." The pot of soup is at the other end of the table, diagonally in front of Murai, so I pass the bowl on to her.

"While you're at it," I say, and quickly finish what's left in the bottom of my own bowl before handing it to her.

"Even so," Mikami says, "thirty thousand is ridiculous. No wonder everybody skips out." He holds his soup bowl out to Murai. "Fill me up, too, will you?"

"Some places do seem to pay better than others," Yamada says. "It can apparently vary quite a bit from one company to another, depending on where you get sent. And I've heard women get paid better than men do." She picks up a chicken thigh in one hand and literally rips off a bite with her teeth.

"Is that because the women aren't as likely to run away?"

"I suppose. And also because they think they might become mistresses."

"For who?" I ask.

"Who else? The owners of the small businesses that sponsor them."

"You hear about how some of the owners just go from one trainee mistress to the next," says Kishimoto.

"It's a wonder she didn't run away," Murai adds.

"Apart from the low pay, it sounded like her employer was relatively reasonable about other things," Mikami says. "I guess she even managed to work somewhere else in the evening."

"You can do that?" Ito says as he starts refilling his two neighbors' rice bowls.

"Not officially, I'm sure," Mikami shakes his head. "She supposedly wants to go back."

"You mean as a trainee?" I say.

"It'd be nice if there were some other way for them to go, but the trainee system is all there is. Unless you have some special skill," Yamada says, and goes back to gnawing on the thighbone to try to get the last little bits of meat clinging to it. She's going at it as if she might devour the bone itself.

"The boss seems to like her," Mikami says.

"I bet he'll make her a very attractive offer," I say, fixing Mikami in the eye with a look that says, *And what's it to you?*

"By the way, has anybody heard anything about our friend who skipped off to Japan?" Murai asks.

"Maybe she just won't come back," Kishimoto says.

"Nah, she just lets you think that, and then all of a sudden one day she'll show up again," Mikami snorts.

Yamada looks at the women across the table. "You two are coming up on a year pretty soon. Do you still plan to go home at that point?"

Kishimoto and Murai arrived on the same day, from the same Japanese language teacher training institute.

Of the Japanese staff, Hayashi and Yamada have been at the center the longest, and the next longest is me. Everybody else arrived within the last year. Kishimoto and Murai have been here for nine months, Mikami for six, and Ito and Miyahara for three. There's constant turnover, with someone new arriving to fill the gap every time a teacher goes home. The vast majority stay for a year. Once in a while, somebody has so much trouble adapting that they experience some kind of breakdown and go home almost right away.

"That's the plan."

"But we might come back."

"Because of your boyfriends?"

"Uh-huh. Though who knows whether that'll last?"

"Our boyfriends are part of it, but also, we figure we'll just be bored in Japan. Right?" Kishimoto says, turning to Murai for her assent.

"I'm trying to recall why you two decided to come to Vietnam in the first place," Yamada says. "Now that I think of it, I guess maybe I never asked." She doesn't actually sound all that interested in hearing their answers.

"Oh, I don't know," Kishimoto says. "I suppose because you can't experience the real satisfaction of teaching Japanese unless you teach outside the country."

"My, my. A surprisingly high-minded response," Yamada says in a mocking tone.

"Surprisingly? What's that supposed to mean?" Kishimoto sounds offended.

"I was only teasing. Sorry, sorry." She turns to Murai. "How about you?"

"Well . . . If you want the truth, you have to promise not to make fun."

"I promise, I promise. After all, none of us came to this country with any special conviction or sense of mission."

"How do you know that?" I ask.

"Oh, you can tell when you talk to people." She turns back to Murai. "So?"

"Well," she says, making a sheepish expression, "I was actually inspired by watching an old TV show called *Duc*."

"*Duc*?" I say. "You mean as in Viet and Duc, the conjoined twins?"

"No, no, no. Yikes. You really don't know the show?"

"How long ago was it on?"

"Seven, eight years ago, maybe."

"Oh, no wonder. I probably wasn't in Japan at the time. So the story's set here in Vietnam?"

"It's actually about a Japanese teacher here."

"Oh, now I remember! I heard about it. With Narumi Yasuda, if I recall."

"That's right, that's right. And Shingo Katori played a Vietnamese cyclo driver."

"As if you'd ever actually see a cyclo driver built like him," Mikami scoffs.

"If you've never seen it, I recorded it, so I can lend you the tapes," Murai says.

"You brought them with you?"

"You better believe I did. Shingo Katori's so hot."

We hail a passing waiter, and each of us orders something to drink. He writes it all down on a slip of paper. He seems to be rather slow, and I suspect he's going to get the orders wrong even after writing them down.

For rice, the final tally comes to three helpings each for Ito and Yamada, while the rest of us stop at two. For soup it is one bowl only for Kishimoto, but two for everybody else. Even so, we have failed to empty either the rice basin or the soup pot.

Yamada looks at Ito. "This is your first time in Vietnam, too, right?"

"Yes."

"So what inspired you to come here?"

He hesitates. "I hope you won't be disgusted with me," he finally says.

"Why does everybody think they have to preface their answer like that?" Yamada says. "Did you get in trouble with the law and have to get out of the country or something?"

"What a terrible thing to say!" Murai gasps.

"You think so? Even with all the fugitives and ex-cons we know are hiding out in Southeast Asia?"

"You can rest assured I'm not one of them. I just . . . I just heard that the women are pretty and they like Japanese men."

"I see. Sounds like an honest answer."

"Honesty is my only virtue," he says, wiping the sweat from his brow with a hand towel.

Mikami is silently staring off into the distance beyond the terrace.

"And how about you," Murai says, looking at me, a little impishly. "Why did you come to Vietnam?"

"For the food."

I answer at once with a smile, but I can feel Yamada's
eyes on me. I know she has sensed the truth.

"No! You're kidding! You really like Vietnamese food
that much?"

Yes, I'm kidding. The truth is that so long as it was
somewhere outside of Japan, I didn't care where I went.
When I talked to a friend about wanting to leave, she put
me in touch with the boss here, and that's what decided it.

Even though I decided to come here with hardly any
thought, once I arrived, I knew I'd done the right thing.
My salvation was the climate, which keeps it consistently
hot through all four seasons. Climate has a greater influence on our mental state than we might imagine. The
powerful sunshine that beats down day after day here is
bursting with life-affirming energy.

And besides, it's important to carve out a refuge for
yourself. Then, at those times when you find yourself paralyzed and unable to move forward, you can take sanctu-
ary in that safety zone, in order to protect yourself. People
may say you shouldn't run away, but if you end up dying
because you failed to flee, then it's all over for you. *You
died only because you were weak. It was simply unavoidable,*
they may try to tell you, but that's not necessarily true.
Maybe if you'd fled the place and gone somewhere else,
you could have lived on.

So ultimately, you have to think it through for yourself.

The waiter comes back and thumps our many-colored drinks on the table, one after the other. Strawberry shake, avocado shake, mango shake, coconut shake, plum juice, iced coffee.

After taking a long slurp of her green shake, Yamada speaks up again. "Basically, none of us finds Japan a very congenial place to live—isn't that what it comes down to? If we loved Japan and found it more hospitable, then we'd never have wanted to leave."

"These days, anybody who says they love Japan so much they never want to leave is probably a bit of a right-winger, wouldn't you say?" Mikami remarks.

"I don't think that's true," Yamada responds, with a faraway look coming into her eyes, as if she's remembering something.

"Well, if you ask me, the country does seem to be leaning further and further to the right," Mikami says, after taking a sip of his iced coffee.

"Do I recall correctly that *this* country is supposed to be on the left?" Murai quips.

"That's easy to forget when you live in Ho Chi Minh City, isn't it?" Kishimoto says.

"Oh, I almost forgot to mention," Yamada says. "Hayashi will be moving to South America soon. He's been accepted into the government's senior volunteers program for overseas Japanese communities."

"Wow!" exclaims Murai. "That man is really something. At sixty-what is he now?"

"He sure doesn't let anything slow him down, does he?" says Ito, who is jabbing his straw into the sugared plums at the bottom of his glass, trying to break them up. "Even here, he's constantly racing about on his motorbike from one class to the next."

"You know, those are yummier when you chomp into them whole instead of breaking them apart," I advise Ito.

"He says he's going to start learning Spanish," Yamada says.

"We can't compete with him. None of us. We should all emulate him more."

Kishimoto and Murai are sipping furiously on their respective red and orange shakes, slurping them up so fast I'm worried they'll end up with brain freezes.

From where we sit, we have a clear view of the motorcycles and pedestrians going back and forth in front of the café. Across the street and to the right is a private high school built during the French colonial period. Some scenes in the movie *The Lover* were filmed there. Students emerge from the building to hop on the back of their parents' motorcycles or to ride off on their own. The tails of the white *ao dai* tunics worn by the girls flutter in the breeze at the school gate and on the backs of motorbikes. These white uniforms present a striking picture from a distance, but when you get up close, you can usually see that the fabric has yellowed, or is noticeably soiled along the hem. A young boy pushing a fruit cart appears from the left and one of the schoolgirls stops him. On the front of the cart is a glass case with an assortment of fruit

spread across a large slab of ice inside. Typically, you tell
the boy what you want, and he cuts it up and places it on
a plastic saucer or in a small plastic bag for you to take
with you. The girl buys some watermelon and papaya.
After paying the boy, she quickly spears a piece of papaya
with a bamboo skewer and pops it into her mouth. The
boy drops the money into his pocket and continues on his
way under the glaring sun. I can see his dusty, sticklike an-
kles protruding beneath the cuffs of his grimy pants. He
appears to be about junior high age, but it's a good bet
that he doesn't go to school. I think about the boy selling
fruit and the girl in the white uniform, and wonder what
their perceptions of each other might be.

SO BROILING HOT IS THE SUN AS WE HEAD BACK TO
the office that I fear any exposed skin on my body might
actually start sizzling. Since Yamada, Mikami, and I are
the only ones with vehicles, each of us takes a colleague
on the back. Yamada rides a large-model scooter, while
Mikami owns a big sport bike.

Riding through town in the open air, odors of every
kind drift by on the breeze—from the smell of fruit, food
carts, and fish sauce to the stench of urine, drainage
ditches, and decaying plants and animals. Some trigger
fond memories; others I've never encountered before.

Driving directly in front of me is a shabby-looking man
on a rusty old Super Cub with about twenty chickens
hanging upside down by their legs from his luggage rack

and handlebars. Every so often, one of them opens its eyes or bends its neck, confirming that the birds are still alive. No doubt the man is delivering them to a market or a restaurant somewhere. I'm amazed at how well his Super Cub runs, even with a muffler rusted full of holes.

Since coming to live in this city, I've discovered the wonder that is the Honda Super Cub. Durable. Reliable. Economical. It's a means of transportation with outstanding resale value, and you routinely see models from as far back as the seventies still running about with the rest. It's fair to say that the Vietnamese fondness for "Made in Japan" started with the company that brought us this machine. Honda has become the generic word for motorized two-wheelers here. Even Yamahas and Suzukis are called Hondas.

I MEET KONNO FOR DINNER ONE NIGHT. HE SAYS HE has a craving for Japanese food and takes me to an *izakaya*-style restaurant. One step inside the door, and I'm surprised to find myself standing in Japan. Wow! I never realized that the favorite hangout of the middle-aged Japanese male had been duplicated in Vietnam, too. The clientele appears to be made up entirely of Japanese businessmen. Since I've spent all my time here going to purely Vietnamese establishments with Yun—especially the kind of local places where foreigners never set foot— I am transfixed by the familiar images of home spread out before me.

"This is amazing!" I gush, trying to convey the extent of my astonishment to Konno. "It's like we're actually in Japan! Every last person here is Japanese!"

"Huh? What do you mean? So what?" he says, clearly not sharing my amazement. I suppose in his circles, he encounters scenes like this all the time.

I continue to marvel over the place as we drink beer and nibble on appetizers of sashimi and salt-cured squid and edamame—mainstays of *izakaya* menus back home that trigger waves of nostalgia in me.

"You don't come to places like this?" he asks.

"No. Never once."

"You always eat Vietnamese?"

"Pretty much."

"I guess you've become so adapted, you're practically one of them."

"You think that might be a bad idea? I like it that nobody tries to take advantage of me."

"You'll have a hard time readjusting when you get back to Japan."

"If I ever go back."

"You like it here that much?"

"It's not as if I'm totally in love with the place, but I think maybe I prefer it to Japan."

"I don't get that. Everything is about money, money, money with these people. There's something perversely intense about the way they worship money. All the cold calculation wears me out."

"Mmm. Because without money, you die."

The people of this city throw themselves into the pursuit of money without the slightest regard for what anybody else might think. To see the single-minded zeal with which they do this takes you past astonishment to a kind of admiration. As certainly as one and one make two, as certainly as the rising sun brings morning, living in this city makes the notion that money is the source of happiness seem like an incontrovertible fact of life. The daughters and sons of poverty-stricken farm families are to this day being sold for income by their parents. The blossoming daughters are forced into prostitution, and younger girls and boys are harvested for their organs.

"It's money over love," Konno says.

"The reason so many people want to marry a foreigner boils down to money, too. And then there's bride brokering."

"They get sold overseas, right? Is it the Taiwanese and Koreans that are the biggest customers these days?"

"That's right. I heard that the buyers are often ex-cons or people with disabilities."

"Currency differences are a big part of it. If you're born where the currency is strong, you may be poor by your own country's standards, but when you convert to the currency of a country like Vietnam, you're not so poor anymore. You can afford to buy a wife."

"Still, I'd rather have a rich Vietnamese husband than a poor Japanese one any day."

"But look at them. They're all nothing but nouveau riche weirdos. We Japanese are much more good-natured, and that's why people like us so much in other countries."

"Like us in *some* other countries. Like the Philippines and Turkey and Mongolia."

"And Vietnam, too."

"Uh-huh. A lot of people do seem to like us here. Maybe it's the Honda effect."

There's a man drinking alone at the counter with his back to us. A powerful aura of homesickness hovers over his bearing.

"I have to make a trip home next week," Konno says as I gaze at the forlorn man's back.

"Oh? Didn't you just go last month? Will it be for longer this time?"

"No. Just three days."

"Is this something that came up suddenly?"

"Uh-huh. There was a bit of a screwup. It's giving me knots in my stomach," he says, frowning.

"Sounds like it must be messy," I say in a somber tone.

"Oh, sorry. I guess this makes me look bad, doesn't it," he says, grinning sheepishly.

"How'd you like to play a game? Bottoms up on Which Way Pop?"

"Huh?"

"We play Which Way Pop, and the loser has to drain his glass."

"I haven't played anything like that in decades."

"So think of it as a chance to return to your youth."

"I'd rather play Yes, Your Majesty."

"That doesn't work with only two people. How about Old New East West then?"

"Do you know the Mitsuo Senda game?"

"You can't play that with just two people either. So, Old New East West it is! Yaay! The Vietnam edition! Whoopee!"

"The Vietnam edition?"

"Uh-huh. Here goes. In times old and new, in lands east and west, *chopitty chop chop*. The topic iiis . . . Vietnamese cities! Ho Chi Minh City! *Chop chop*," I say and clap my hands twice.

"Okay, so I just name a city? Um, Hanoi." This time we both say *chop chop* and clap our hands.

"Da Lat." *Chop chop*.

"Hue." *Chop chop*.

"Nha Chang." *Chop chop*.

"Da Nang." *Chop chop*.

"My Tho." *Chop chop*.

"Hoi An." *Chop chop*.

"Vung Tau." *Chop chop*.

"Umm . . . what was that place called? Ohh, it's on the tip of my tongue . . . um . . . Sa Pa." *Chop chop*.

"Can Tho." *Chop chop*.

"Umm . . .um. . . oh, no, I'm drawing a blank."

"In that case, five, four, three—"

"Oh, I know, Cu Chi." *Chop chop*.

"Tay Ninh." *Chop chop*.

"Tay Ninh?"

"It's where Caodaism has its headquarters. Your turn. Hurry!"

"Umm . . . umm . . ."

"Five, four, three . . ."

"Umm . . ."

". . . two, one! *Bzzzzz!* You lose! *Palila palila palila palila,* drink u-u-up!"

"Oh, man, I forgot about that cheer."

Konno has a hard time getting into the spirit at first, but once he loses three in a row and has three full glasses of beer in him, a hell-bent look comes into his eyes and he becomes determined to beat me. The result, though, is that I keep winning, and he's soon had a lot to drink— which revs him up all the more.

"C'mon. Let's go somewhere else!" he says, and takes me from there to a hostess bar. I want to tell him that I'd actually rather hop into bed than drink, but I can't bring myself to say it.

It's a small place with a mirror ball turning on the ceiling and karaoke music blaring. The singer at the microphone appears to be the only other customer, but there must be ten hostesses, all dressed in colorful *ao dai.* We're shown to a table, where most of the hostesses join us as we sit down. The way Konno starts bantering with the *ao dai* beauties tells me he must be a regular here.

He hands me the book of karaoke songs. "Sing something," he says. Then he pours me some wine. "Have a drink. They say this is courtesy of Mr. Sasaki, who's up there singing right now. It's supposed to be a very good wine."

When he's finished singing, Sasaki joins us at our table. The business card he hands me is imprinted with the logo of a big-name corporation. To judge from the color of his cheeks, he's already had quite a few.

The girl who has ensconced herself next to Konno keeps shooting dirty looks my way. I suppose she has a thing for him. She's obviously very young. She's wearing a red see-through *ao dai* embroidered in gold, which does little to conceal her bra.

All of the hostesses speak some Japanese, but their levels of competence vary widely. The one who sits down next to me and introduces herself as Anh seems to be the oldest among them—though she's still younger than me—as well as the most fluent. I sit talking with her while Konno and his friend throw themselves into round after round of karaoke. Her small face is framed by long, glossy hair falling straight down over her shoulders. She has the slender figure that *ao dai* are made for. Not surprisingly for someone who works in a place like this, she's very pretty.

KONNO IS FALLING-DOWN DRUNK BY THE TIME WE leave, but somehow I manage to drive him back to his apartment on the back of my motorcycle and get him into bed.

After pausing a moment to catch my breath, I go into the kitchen and help myself to a can of cola from the refrigerator before plopping down on the sofa in the living room. It's been a long time since I've had a soda, and the carbonation is like needles in my throat.

I ponder the wide gap that still seems to separate Konno and me. Will this gap naturally fill in over time? Or will that happen only if we make a special effort? Might it just remain always the same, no matter what? Or perhaps even grow wider?

I look up at the moon shining in through the lace curtains. How long has it been since I last saw the moon? I wonder where Yun is tonight. Is she sleeping with Takahashi? To think of Yun having sex with a man doesn't make me burn with jealousy. Quite the contrary—I imagine it would prompt me to pleasure myself. I'd love to see her writhing in bliss from the touch of a man's tongue, or the thrust of his penis deep inside her.

After finishing my drink, I return to the bedroom and crawl into bed next to Konno. He is sleeping soundly, his breath rising and falling in a low snore. Though our skin does not touch, I can feel the heat of his body warming my right side. A man's body is like a furnace. It gives off a warmth that summons sleep.

WE BOTH GET UP NEAR NOON AND FIX OURSELVES A brunch of fried eggs, Vienna sausages, salad, and toast. When we've finished eating, we lie on the sofa watching a

DVD—a recording of a comedy show from Japanese TV. I'm soon wrapped in a world of humor that makes sense only among our fellow Japanese: gags that only the born and raised would understand; rapid-fire lines only a native speaker could catch. I reflect on the vast gap separating the language I teach and the language in current use on Japanese TV.

Konno keeps cracking up. He hasn't said anything, but I know he's noticed that the calls I used to get so frequently from Yun whenever I was with him have ceased.

When the DVD is over, we fill the bath and climb in together.

"I'd sure like to go to a hot springs sometime," I say.

"Do they have them here?"

"Uh-huh. I think not too far from Vung Tau. Though in a place that's kind of hard to get to."

Our bodies are joined under the water. Coupled but motionless. We are both holding completely still, deferring completion, savoring the brink.

I realize that I can take his penis inside me without the slightest hesitation, yet I find myself shying from placing my mouth on his. For it is Yun's lips that I yearn for—that seem the more delectable, the more desirable.

No matter how far I may go with Konno, we will in the end always remain a man and a woman. What I have with him can never bring me the melting and mingling into one that I experienced with Yun. That kind of oneness simply isn't possible with him.

It was a week after Yun left that I stopped texting her

and calling. Three more weeks have subsequently gone by, making it now a full month since I last saw her.

I must resign myself to a life in Ho Chi Minh City that no longer includes Yun. But every place I go in the city is linked to memories of her. As long as I remain here, I can never forget her. No one can replace her. There is no other like her. No one even close.

ANOTHER CALL FROM MY MOTHER. IS THERE NO ESCAPE?

I cannot take on her anger and fears.

She's the one who made the wrong choices in life, and I wish she wouldn't try to blame them on me. How long does she intend to keep moaning that it's because I was born, because she had me, that things were so hard? It's not my fault she has ended up without husband or money. She's the one who chose to live the way she did. Yet without even the tiniest acknowledgment of that fact, she expects me to clean up the mess she's made of her life. She assails me with the same tired old phrase every time she calls: *Is this the thanks I get for raising you?*

My mother was very much the hands-off kind of parent, abdicating any effort to teach me the life skills a child needs to learn. She was constantly saying *It's too much trouble* or *I'm too tired*—and I always took these excuses at face value. I figured any corners she cut must have been because she deserved a little break for having to raise me all by herself.

But my perspective has changed since meeting Yun's

mother. Here is a woman who single-handedly brought up six daughters by pounding the pavement as a peddler—all while living through a war, and without ever receiving any public assistance. What a contrast she is to my own mother, who lived in a country undisturbed by war, worked in the comfort of an office, and was able to draw on public assistance when she needed it, as she raised her only child.

When I compare these two women, Yun's mother looms as a figure of great dignity. She sits there like a rock, creating a sense of balance for her family. She has confidence, she has a clear sense of herself, and she has convictions. And therefore she represents security and stability.

None of these things can be said about my mother. That's precisely why I find her so aggravating.

When I compare the imposing presence of Yun's mother with my own mother's craven and desperate efforts to hide her want of confidence, it leads me to only one conclusion: my mother was woefully lacking in any ability to teach or positively influence a child. And I think ultimately this was because she herself had no idea how to determine what was right and what was wrong.

My mother was never quite able to catch the current of the times in an era when values were changing day by day, and, in effect, she ended up dead in the water. Legions of men and women like her can be found in Japan today, driving themselves to illness, or even suicide.

.   .   .   .

ONE NIGHT, KANAZAWA TAKES ME TO ONE OF HIS
regular bars. American rock music is playing loudly in the
dimly lit room. The patrons are mostly white males,
along with some Asian men who look like they must be
Taiwanese. At the back of the room is a billiard table
where several hulking men are drinking beer and shooting pool.

We sit down side by side at one end of the bar, and the
bartender comes to take our orders. There are in fact two
bartenders—one who looks American, the other Vietnamese. Kanazawa seems to know them both well.

Every so often, the American performs moves reminis-
cent of Tom Cruise in the movie *Cocktail* as he serves bar
patrons. At one of the tables behind us, a group of people
I take to be Americans are having a roaring good time. My
eyes vaguely follow the action on the TV at the right end
of the bar, where a soccer game is in progress. Three
stools over, a middle-aged Caucasian man with a belly is
being approached by an aging hooker in frighteningly
heavy makeup and a garish open-backed dress. The
younger and prettier hookers have already been claimed
for the night, but this woman hasn't been able to find any
takers, and panic seems to be setting in. With fresh young
girls arriving by the day from the countryside, the city is
overflowing with prostitutes; I'm surprised a woman like
her can even survive amid the competition.

A waitress in a provocative uniform comes by to ask
Kanazawa if she can get us anything to eat. Just then a
tall, drunken American perches himself on the stool be-

side me and immediately starts bad-mouthing the Vietnamese.

"If you feel that way, then maybe it's time for you to go
home," I suggest, trying my best to modulate the tone of
my voice. "I'm not really interested in your complaints."

He throws me a startled look before staggering off
toward the pool table, muttering something under his
breath.

A couple at the table directly behind me have been carrying on an extended argument—a white man with Latin
features, and a Vietnamese woman who evidently is not a
prostitute. She is trying desperately to patch things up
with the man in her heavily accented beginner's English.
He responds coldly, obviously having tired of her. He's
probably thinking, *Now that we've had a good time, I want to
move on,* while she's thinking, *Now that we've had a good
time, I want to get married.* She's determined not to let her
chance of catching a foreign husband slip away.

Stupid woman, I think to myself, and it makes me sad.
Can't she see that she'll never find happiness by marrying
a loser like him?

I really do feel sorry for the women in this country.
They're given so little worth. And too many of them
blindly internalize this attitude and treat themselves ac-
cordingly. Yet these same women are also so strong and
indomitable. Behind this apparent paradox lies the long
shadow of the war.

"Can I ask you something?" Kanazawa says, out of the
blue. "Do you like women?"

His direct question catches me completely off guard, and the peanut I've just tossed into my mouth goes down whole.

"Huh? What do you mean?" I try playing dumb.

"Somehow I get that feeling from you."

"Are you saying you think you can recognize your own type?"

With a sly smile tugging at his lips, Kanazawa tosses a peanut in the air and tilts his head back to catch it in his mouth.

"There aren't that many gay men here, are there?" I say. "Thailand has so many more. Why did you come to Vietnam?"

"You think I'm gay?"

"Aren't you?"

"Hardly," he says as if he can't imagine where I could have gotten such a crazy idea. He tilts his head right and left to crack his neck.

"Well, you do come off that way, you know."

"That's . . . problematic."

He knows that I see right through his lie.

A guy who comes up to the bar to get a drink stops to say hello to Kanazawa. It's obvious that they know each other.

"This is Jim. He's from England," Kanazawa says. "He used to teach English in Japan, around four years ago."

Kanazawa's Englishman friend is the so-called handsome type. There was a time when I was highly enamored of men like him. I thought I was so superior just for having someone like that as a boyfriend. Talk about stupid. But everybody around me was the same—always getting envious or intimidated when they learned I had an Anglo-Saxon boyfriend with white skin and blond hair and gray eyes. I could feel the difference in how people looked at me as we walked around Tokyo together. Their eyes were filled with a combination of yearning and inferiority and self-abasement. But in truth, the man had come running to the Far East with his tail between his legs: he was a loser.

Losers from the developed countries wash up on the shores of Asia. They can be found inhabiting nearly every part of the continent, taking full advantage of their cachet as foreigners.

CHAPTER SEVEN

ON MY WAY HOME AFTER FINISHING up for the day, I stop for some noodles at one of my favorite food stalls. The lady who operates the place isn't particularly friendly, but she makes a good bowl of noodles.

As I sip some coconut water after I'm done eating, I gaze at the lights brightening the row of stalls set up along the street. Beggars stop in front of me from time to time with their hands extended. I mimic the locals and resolutely ignore them. I think about how Yun would handle the situation better if she were here.

I am reluctant to go on home to my empty apartment, where my solitude will feel so much more complete. But Konno is busy entertaining a visitor from Japan who arrived a couple of days ago, and when I think of spending the time with anyone else, I decide I'd rather be alone. Most weekdays I can distract myself with preparations for the next day, but tomorrow is Sunday.

I drive around town for a brief while before resigning myself to the inevitable and heading home. After taking a shower, I crawl languidly into bed and watch a VCD that Cham lent me. It's an episode of *Takeshi's Castle.* I remember watching the show as a teenager in Japan when it was originally broadcast. Fifteen years or so later, I had a chance to see some recordings of it when I was in Australia, and then again in Thailand. With its easily grasped premise, the show was hugely popular among the local viewers. Even after a decade and a half, I found that its appeal had not faded in the least.

I hear a bike drive up and the motor shut off. It's followed by the sounds of somebody returning home and Cham opening the gate. If that's Kanazawa, I think to myself, maybe I'll see about borrowing a book to read.

Suddenly there's a knock at my door. Since I'm not expecting anyone, it makes me jump. I go to the door and call out, "*A-i?* (Who is it?)"

There's a pause. "Yun."

I catch my breath at the sound of the familiar husky voice coming through the door. I stand paralyzed, uncertain what to do.

"Hiro?"

Yun's voice comes again, and it jolts me back to my senses. I take a deep breath, then open the door. She's standing there with her head bent and a baseball-style cap pulled down over her eyes, so I can't see her face. For several moments, neither of us says anything. My head is a complete blank. I simply stare at the tiny figure standing before me.

"May I come in?" she finally says in a low voice.

I let her into the room and close the door.

She fidgets as she sits down on the end of the bed and removes her hat. I sit next to her, waiting to hear what she has to say. On TV, a contestant is making her way across a hanging bridge, trying not to get knocked off by the flying volleyballs being shot at her.

"Are you angry, Hiro?" Yun asks, staring at the screen.

"No, I'm not angry," I say, looking directly at her face. She still won't meet my eyes.

"I think about many things."

"Uh-huh."

"I think . . ."

All of a sudden her eyes fill and tears roll down her cheeks. I lift my hand and stroke her hair.

"Did Takahashi dump you?"

"What?" she asks, looking at me for the first time since arriving at my door. Her eyes are like those of a scared animal. Seeing them, I realize my attack instinct has been awakened.

"Did you and Takahashi say goodbye?"

"He . . . he has girlfriend in Japan," she says slowly, in a tear-filled voice, and I feel my irritation rising.

"Is that why you came back to me?"

There's a pause before she answers. "No. Because I love you."

"But you wouldn't be here now if Takahashi didn't have a girlfriend. Isn't that right?" I say, in deliberately acid tones.

"I not know," she whispers.

"You know very well! You ignored every message I sent, and every time I called! You left me without any explanation! And then when you break up with Takahashi, you think you can just come running back to me? Isn't that expecting an awful lot?"

"Like I think before, you are angry."

"Did you ever stop to think about my feelings?"

The shrinking look in her eyes is wiped away by a combative flash. "What about my feelings? Did you think? My feelings when you go to see Konno-san, and I am waiting, all alone. Did you think then?"

I say nothing.

"Always you are first to do!" she continues.

"So you're saying it's my fault?"

"It's better if I never meet you! It's better if I know only men!"

"You want to say goodbye to me?"

"I want to, but I cannot do. Because I love you, more than anybody," she says, and presses her lips to mine.

"Why?" I ask, as I gently nibble at her lips. They are so soft and sweet. I've missed these lips. Tasting them again fills me with desire.

"Because you love me so much. Nobody love me so much like you."

Yun smiles. That cutest, most adorable of smiles. With one flash of that smile, I'm ready to forgive everything. And I feel an overwhelming desire to make that smile my own.

I DRINK A MANGO SHAKE AT HAI'S CAFÉ WHILE I wait for Yun. With each sip, the thick liquid washes across my tongue and the rich, tangy sweetness of mango spreads through my mouth.

Trieu is reading a newspaper at the table next to me and Hai peers over his shoulder to offer a remark about something. I often run into him here, catching up on the day's developments over coffee. When something big happens, or when there's news from Japan, he kindly fills me in on what the paper reports.

Trieu looks to be in his upper thirties. He has a low-paying job, domineering wife, and two unruly children. Along the jawline of his dark-complexioned face is a large mole with four or five long black hairs growing from it. The longest of them is about five centimeters long. Mole hairs are considered lucky in this country, a symbol of wealth, so you're supposed to leave them unplucked. That's presumably why you see such an inordinate number of people here with hairs growing out of moles. Every now and then I even encounter women who are letting such hairs grow. At any rate, whenever I look at

Trieu, my eyes tend to be drawn to those hairs. I try not to
let him notice that I'm staring.

He glances at the cheap-looking gold watch on his
wrist, quickly swallows the rest of his coffee, and holds
his newspaper out to me.

"Would you like to read it?" he asks.

When I take the paper, he stands, hops onto the clunky
Chinese-made motorcycle parked in front of his table,
nods goodbye, and slowly putters away.

Sometimes I've noticed Trieu eyeing me suggestively. I
sense in his gaze that deep-seated lustfulness common to
all men, which gives their eyes a certain oily sheen. Back
in Japan, I used to experience feelings of deep disgust
when I encountered that greasy sheen in crowded trains
or on the street or at drinking houses. But my intense re-
vulsion to it has softened since seeing that my own reflection in Yun's eyes had the same shine.

I scan the newspaper. Since I lack a big enough vocabu-
lary to read whole articles with any ease, I rely on the
photos and pick out words and phrases I recognize to try
to get a general sense of the content. The bird flu out-
break continues to spread across the country. . . . Last
night in Ho Chi Minh City, a bus plowed into five motorcycles, killing two people. . . . Today the police will . . . do
something, but I can't make it out.

My mango shake is gone, so I ask Hai for some tea. She
points her chin to signal that I should get it myself. Since
I'm her only customer at the moment, she's taking the
opportunity to give the concrete pavement a once-over

with her bamboo broom. I rise to get my tea. Behind a dingy glass case that holds sweets and cigarettes is an old wooden stand with a deep, dark patina that gives it the air of a real antique. This is where the tea leaves, coffee beans, and hot-water thermos are kept. Sometimes when things get so busy that Hai can't keep up, she calls out, "Could you get us a coffee over here, Hiro?" and I come here to prepare the order and take it to the customer. While I'm brewing the tea, Hai quickly sweeps the pavement around my table.

When I come back and sit down, she drops into the chair next to mine. "Yun's awfully late today," she says.

Her remark makes me realize it's late even by Yun's standards. I text her and immediately get a reply.

"Bike is broken. Come pick up please."

Great. In that case, why didn't she call?

"Her motorbike broke down. She needs me to pick her up," I say as I get to my feet and pay Hai.

"Oh, dear," she says without sounding particularly surprised. Then she slaps me on the rump and says, "Better get moving, then."

THE GATE ATTENDANT WHERE YUN WORKS KNOWS me well, so he greets me with a smile and lets me right in.

"I'm here," I text, and moments later Yun emerges from her building with Tan, my former neighbor. Tan waves at me and hurries off toward the parking lot.

"What's wrong with your bike?" I ask

"Brakes stop working. It's fixing now."

"That seems unusual for a Japanese bike."

"It go crash."

"What? You had an accident? Are you all right?"

"Not had an accident. Bike fall down in parking lot."

"Oh. That's a relief."

"You worry?" she asks with a contented smile.

"Hop on. I'm starving."

"I want to eat goat tonight."

"Goat? So that place by the market?"

"Yes, go there, please," she says, then hops lightly onto my rear seat and wraps her arms around my waist.

"Is Tan coming, too?"

"No, Tan is busy."

THE RESTAURANT IS HAZY WITH SMOKE AND HOPPING with customers and waiters.

"How did it go last night?"

As I start putting pieces of goat's udder on the charcoal grill, I ask about the outing she had with some teachers from her school.

"I get very tired."

"Did you have fun?"

"You not there, so a little bit fun. If you there, it is much more fun."

"Right, right," I say. "So how many people did you go with? Did the teachers eat much?"

Yun is choosing not to help with the food, so I get to be the grill master.

"Oh, yes! The teachers eat many, many helpings. After we eat, we all go to coffee shop. Um, eight people go."

"Wow. It was a big group."

I divide the cooked meat between Yun's dipping bowl and mine.

"You want to marry someone Japanese, right?" I say. "I can't marry you, you know."

"Yes, I know."

I've put too much meat in her bowl, so she moves several pieces to mine and motions with her chin for me to eat them. I dutifully start in on the small pile of goat morsels in my bowl, chewing mechanically.

"You eat the rest," I say.

"No more for you? You like goat's udder, yes?"

"I like the taste, but I just can't eat very much meat."

"You have big chest, so you can be grill like this," she says with a wicked grin, "but my chest too small. Nothing to grill." Her lips glisten with the oils from the meat.

"But it'd be all fat, so it wouldn't taste very good."

"You want to drink something?"

"Coconut water."

Stacking the rest of the meat in Yun's bowl, I tell our waiter that we're done grilling. He brings a deep earthenware pot and places it on our charcoal burner. The pot is filled with broth in which goat's meat is already simmering, and I dump the vegetables in on top. Yun is still busy with her grilled meat, so I'm the cook again.

"Yesterday you go to see Konno-san?"

"Uh-huh."

"I not like when you go to see him."

"Uh-huh."

"But still you go to see him, yes?"

"Uh-huh."

"It's not fair."

"Uh-huh."

"Hmph. You say only uh-huh, uh-huh, uh-huh. It's not nice."

"Sorry."

"You like Konno-san, yes?"

"I like him very much. He's a nice man."

"Only like? Or love?"

I stir the pot with the mini soup ladle as I think about it. "Hmm . . ."

"You will become his girlfriend?"

"Hmm . . ."

"Who you like more? Konno-san or me?"

"Hmm . . . The thing is, how I like you and how I like him are so different."

"Then which for me? Love? Or like?"

"Hmm . . ."

"Which?"

"That's a real conundrum."

"Conundrum?"

"It means it's a difficult question. But I guess . . . well . . . I guess the answer is love," I finally conclude. "Since we say 'I love you' to our families, too."

"In that case, *yen* (romantic love)? Or *thoung* (familial love)?"

"This is hard. I don't know . . . Hmm. What about for you? Which am I—*yen* or *thoung*?"

"I not know too. . . . But, maybe *thoung,* I think."

"I see."

It's a little bit of a shock. I think.

"I want you to stay in Vietnam longest time."

"You mean until I die?"

"Yes, yes, you must die in Vietnam. But not die before me."

"Why not?"

"If you die, I am too lonely!"

"But if you die first, then I'll be the lonely one! And in an alien land!"

"Alien land?"

"A foreign country."

"Oh. Then after I die, you must go home to Japan."

"Huh? How's that supposed to work? I wind up back in Japan at sixty or seventy with no job and no pension."

Yun giggles, with a crooked smile.

I SEE KONNO FROM TIME TO TIME, TOO. HE'S A BUSY man, so it's not all that often that we can get together, but even so, when I tell Yun I'm going out with him, she makes it unmistakably clear that she doesn't like it. She sulks like a child and even tries to make me call off my plans by pretending to be sick when I'm about to leave.

With Konno, I deliberately maintain a certain distance. The physical part of our relationship is fine, but I want to avoid getting too deeply attached emotionally. Yet I'm also loath to lose him. I'm afraid that if I forget that distinctively masculine smell, or if I lose the sensation of his penis inside me, then I'll no longer be a woman. And I so want to go on loving Yun as a woman.

A FEW DAYS BEFORE THE STUDENTS IN MY TRAINEE class are scheduled to depart for Japan, we all go out to lunch together. Phuc, who co-teaches with me, comes along too. We head out on a slew of motorcycles and travel in formation to Thanh Da. Clouds of dust billow behind us as we proceed along the unpaved country roads.

When we arrive, the restaurant has tables and chairs arranged around a large pond in the middle—an artificial pond that's simply been carved out of the ground—with a roof over the seating area for shade. The idea is that you fish for your dinner in the pond and then eat what you catch. The students drop their lines in the water as soon as we arrive. Phuc and I and several of the students who aren't so young anymore watch the others from the shade, sipping lemonade.

A variety of small trees dot the grounds, and I see a dog sleeping in the shade of one, looking dead to the world. Beyond the trees are rice paddies, brimming with water and reflecting the intense sunlight. When I gaze a little too long at the brightly glittering surfaces, I begin to feel dizzy. My lungs fill with the fresh smell of earth and trees and water and, lifting my eyes, I see a massive white column of cloud rising brilliantly against the pure blue sky. The sun pours down on the parched, reddish brown earth, and on the palm trees and yellow flowers that sway gently in the light breeze.

The students catch several large fish, which soon return from the kitchen steamed whole, in crisp-fried pieces, and sliced up for fish-and-vegetable hot pots. The students wait hand and foot on Phuc and me. She's well accustomed to being treated this way by her students and not the least bit shy about telling them what to do. "Give me some more soup," she orders, or "Go ask for some hand cloths." The meal is, of course, the students' treat. No matter how poor, a student always makes sure the teacher does not have to pay. My students frequently invite me to go places with them, and they're always uncommonly pleased when I accept. In this country you often get special treatment just for being a teacher, especially if you're a foreigner. According to Konno, I'm getting to experience the most appealing side of the Vietnamese people. In his business, he apparently has to deal with plenty of nasty, crafty types, and sometimes he gets thoroughly fed up with them. I guess he's right that my experience is one-sided.

"Sensei, Japan is hotch now, or Japan is cold now?"

"Japan is very cold now. Because it's winter."

Will these students really be able to endure the chill of

Japan's winters? I worry especially about the ones being sent north of Tokyo, to Gunma.

"By the way, everybody, I'm sure you are all excited about going to Japan. But I want you to know that life there may not be easy for you."

"Yes. It's no problem."

"We work very hard."

"No, really, I'm serious about this. The companies you go to work for can turn out to be bad companies. Sometimes the boss is a bad person."

"It's no problem, Sensei. You are worried for us?" Chan sounds amused.

I don't know whether he gets it or not—or if it makes no difference because he intends to take off on his own once he gets there. Yeah, I bet that's the plan—at least for someone like Chan. He's probably already got everything set up with the Vietnamese syndicate in Japan. That look on his face seems to say, *I'm ready to roll.* I can't see the faintest shadow of doubt or anxiety in it.

"Chan-san," I say, "when you come back to Vietnam after Japan, what will you do?"

"I buy house. I make company."

"That sounds very good."

Will I ever be able to afford a house, I wonder. Outside the major cities, you can buy a house for the equivalent of a few million yen in this country. But Ho Chi Minh City is in the midst of a housing bubble that's sent prices soaring to absurd levels—to tens and hundreds of million yen. Property values are no different from Tokyo, in a city where a cup of coffee costs twenty yen and a full lunch just fifty yen.

SEVERAL DAYS LATER I GO TO THE AIRPORT TO SEE my students off. Dressed up in suits they're not accustomed to, with neckties pulled tight around their collars, they all look uncomfortably stiff. Some are in tears as they say goodbye to their families, while others are all smiles. They will not get to come home for three full years. I wonder how their opinion of Japan will have changed by the time they return to this airport three years down the road.

All I can do for them now is to hope and pray that the employers they've been placed with will treat them honorably.

SUNDAY NEAR NOON. ANOTHER CLEAR DAY. I CAN feel the sun piercing right through my clothes to my skin as I drive toward Konno's condo. He has learned to recognize me coming, even in my total-body protective gear that would do a bank robber proud.

My Super Cub has just been serviced and the engine is humming smoothly. The instruments and blinkers remain nonfunctional as always, so I have to use hand signals when turning or changing lanes. I simply hold my arm down at an angle and stir the air with my hand to tell the vehicles behind me I intend to move over. Signaling is generally considered the responsibility of the passenger on the back, so when Konno is riding with me, it becomes his job. It didn't take him long to learn how and when he needed to signal. Ideally, the passenger should not just sit passively, but anticipate every change of direction— checking with the driver when necessary, as well as keeping tabs on the motorcycles to the right and left and behind—to help steer his ride efficiently along the most desirable trajectory. Needless to say, I manage all this entirely on my own when I'm riding solo, but because it's so small, my bike is considerably harder to handle with a passenger aboard—especially one of Konno's size—and it takes all my strength on the handlebars to keep it from wobbling out of control. I need to avoid driving with one hand or taking my eyes off the road in front of me any more than I absolutely have to, so it helps a lot when the person on the back pitches in. The teamwork also fosters a feeling of togetherness.

"Right at the next corner," I call back to Konno as we make our way toward the Diamond Plaza Department Store in District 1. "Straight ahead here." It takes us less than five minutes to get there from his building.

First on our agenda is lunch at the Korean restaurant on the second floor. The other diners are all Korean. I order the stone-baked beef-and-vegetable *bibimbap*. Konno chooses a fish stew. His forehead beads up with sweat as he mutely works his way through the piping-hot bowl. When he's finished with that, he decides he's still hungry and orders some seafood pancakes.

"There's something I wanted to ask you," he says as he takes a sip of the sweet mint tea that came with his meal. "About the Japanese language test—the one foreigners take to show how much Japanese they know. You know, like the test people take in Japan to show how much English they know."

"You mean the Japanese Language Proficiency Test?"

"Probably, yeah. How good is somebody who's passed Level Three?"

"They've probably finished basic Japanese."

"So Level Two would be intermediate?"

"More or less."

"I'm looking to add another person to my staff, so I put out a job ad, and now I've been reading resumes, but I'm not getting anybody who has Level Two."

"Well, that's not surprising, considering that even a lot of experienced Japanese language teachers haven't taken Level Two in this country. Go to China, and you'll find tons of Level Ones, but here in Ho Chi Minh City even Level Twos are a rarity."

"No wonder."

"But you can find people who have an intermediate competence even if they don't have Level Two certification. You just have to interview them and give them a test of your own."

"Could I maybe get you to do that for me?"

"A test?"

"Yeah, I mean, I wouldn't have a clue how to judge."

"How many people are we talking about?"

"Ten. Sorry to spring it on you like this, but I'm hoping to make a decision by a week from today."

"Well, the tricky part will be scheduling. It'll either have to be in the evenings, or else next Sunday."

"I hate to ask you to give up your day off, but can you do it on Sunday?"

"It's going to cost you," I joke, but Konno takes me seriously and tells me in a low voice that I should work up an estimate for him later.

After lunch, we browse the DVD shop on the same floor. Even here, at a shop inside an upscale department store, the VCDs and DVDs on sale are nearly all bootlegs. The newest movies from the United States, Korea, and elsewhere get duplicated and appear in stores right away. Konno buys a dozen or so. Next we go to the video arcade on the fourth floor and play a few rounds of some old classics like Time Crisis and Daytona USA and Puyo Pop.

On our way home we drop by the market to buy food for dinner later on. Konno tags quietly along behind me. Mixed among the stalls selling meat and vegetables and fruit and rice and seasonings and coffee are ones selling dishes and pans and shoes and clothing. This market has a pronounced spicy, fishy, dank odor.

"Sensei!" One of my students calls out to me and approaches with a smile. "*Konnichi wa.* (Hello.)"

"Oh, hello, Ngan-san."

"Do you go shopping, Sensei?"

Ngan is in one of my corporate classes. She always

seems to enjoy the class, participating actively and asking questions.

"Yes."

"What will you buy?"

"I will buy vegetables and chicken. And you?"

"Um, I will buy . . . oh, no . . . I *bought* fruit."

"I see."

Ngan indicates Konno with her eyes and asks with a suggestive smile, "He is your boyfriend?" I smile back ambiguously. "Oh, Sensei. Please take these. Please eat them. They taste delicious."

She holds out the fruit she's just bought. I get this surprisingly often here. My instinct is to turn down offers like this, but people make such sad faces when I do that I've learned to accept the gifts graciously.

"Thank you," I say.

She leans in so only I can hear and whispers, "Your boyfriend is very handsome," then waves goodbye as she walks away.

"You seem to run into your students a lot," Konno says as he watches her go. The time I felt most embarrassed was when some students saw me riding my motorcycle with him on the back.

"It's a crowded city," I say.

Back at Konno's apartment we watch a DVD and then have sex. Afterward, I fix dinner. At his request, I make a Japanese-style simmered dish and a stir-fry. Konno can't cook—or rather, he won't. And even apart from cooking, I've been picking up signs lately that he'd like to rely on me to deal with other domestic things as well. Basically, he's so worn out from working in unfamiliar surroundings that he just wants somebody to take care of him. Which is exactly why I've been carefully maintaining my distance. To make sure he never crosses a certain line, I've drawn a border around myself. I get the sense that he's aware of this border, too.

While we're eating, the usual call from Yun arrives.

"I'm at Konno's. We're having dinner right now. Huh? Now? I don't know. Hold on." I move the phone away from my face and look at Konno. "Yun's saying she'd like to come over. If it's all right."

"It's fine by me."

"Are you sure? You can say no if you want."

"No, really, it's fine."

It's hard to gauge how he really feels, but I tell Yun that it's okay.

Twenty minutes later she arrives. All three of us sit down in the living room. Yun and Konno have met a number of times before, but they've never really said much to each other. Even though her purpose in joining us is to interfere, she shows no sign of harboring any hostility or hatred toward Konno; if anything, she has adopted a friendly attitude toward him. Today, for some reason, she seems embarrassed, while Konno sits there looking unhappy and saying nothing.

He turns to me. "Would she like some beer?"

"You don't want beer, do you, Yun? I'll go get her some juice, if it's all right."

"Sure. Help yourself from the fridge."

I find a carton of orange juice in the refrigerator and pour some into a glass. When I set it down in front of her, Yun turns to me with a smile.

"I want to eat Japanese food," she says, pointing at the large serving platter in the middle of the table.

"Are you sure? I thought you didn't like Japanese food."

"I want to try."

I spoon some onto a small plate for her, and she takes a bite.

"It's very sweet," she says. "Why Japanese food always so sweet?"

"Actually, this isn't as sweet as sometimes. I skipped the sugar."

Konno's eyes are on the TV, but I get the sense that he's actually listening to our exchange.

There have been a number of times recently when I've been with Konno and Yun has crashed the party. I can tell that Konno is gradually warming up to her—to her personality and to the things she says and does. They've gotten so they do exchange a few words now and then. It's an odd sort of triangle. Might Konno even have guessed the nature of my relationship with Yun?

I go home with Yun rather than staying over with Konno. We chat back and forth as we ride side by side through the night.

"Konno-san is nice man, and very handsome. Why not he married?"

"I think he was just always too busy with work."

"You want to marry Konno-san, Hiro?"

I pause. "No, I couldn't."

"Because you love me?" she says, turning to look at me with a beaming smile.

AFTER TET, THE YEAR'S BIGGEST EVENT, CELEBRAT-ing the Vietnamese New Year, there start to be days here and there when I don't see Yun. She explains that her family is dealing with some problems, so she needs to spend the night at home instead of at my apartment. When she does stay with me, she is as eager as ever to make love, and the passion of her embraces remains unchanged. She even seems to be growing more responsive to my touch, and I find myself almost frightened by the levels of ec-stasy she seems to reach.

I sometimes notice her looking at me as if she has something to say. But when I prompt her with my eyes to go ahead, her only response is a weak smile.

On those evenings when she isn't with me, I choose to spend the time alone. I've always had an affinity for soli-tude. When I lived in Japan, I used to keep to myself a great deal. But the sense of isolation I experienced there, in my homeland, was nothing compared to what I experi-ence here, in a foreign country. That's why I'm so amazed by people who can make it entirely on their own when they live abroad.

Until not very long ago, I could always tell how sad Yun became when I was away. Like a baby bird that misses its mother. But these days, my absence no longer seems to bring her such sadness. And that makes *me* feel sad. Even when we are together, I sometimes feel as though her mind is somewhere else. I get the sense that she's not really looking at me. That her heart is slowly starting to drift away. That I'm losing hold of something. Or that there's something I may have thought I held but actually did not. But I tell myself I'm probably just thinking too much, jumping to the wrong conclusions, making things up in my head.

Every so often I'm seized with a desire to see Konno, but he's always busy and it never seems to work out.

AS THE DRY SEASON GIVES WAY TO THE WET, KISHI-moto and Murai finish their year of work and depart for Japan. I go to the airport to say goodbye. They both appear to be in such high spirits that I feel a twinge of envy. I can't imagine myself being so excited when the time comes for me to return home.

I've made the ten-minute trip to the airport a good many times now to see people off: teachers returning to Japan, friends who came to visit me and see the sights, my trainee students on their way to job assignments, Yun's two sisters, and a Vietnamese colleague at the center departing for the United States to get married.

On my way back from the airport, I see a bicycle-drawn cart piled high with coconuts at the side of the road. I stop to buy one, and suck the coconut water from the shell with a straw on the spot.

The coconut water tastes like Yun. The subtle sweetness. The subtle fragrance.

I raise my eyes to the sky as a plane roars overhead.

Perhaps it was to experience this taste that I came here, I think to myself.

Even after ten at night, the temperature remains uncomfortably warm. Thick, sticky air clings to my skin. Soon we will be entering the hottest season of the year. Once again I'm about to plunge into those white-hot days when I feel like even my brain is going to melt away.

CHAPTER EIGHT

"HIRO! IT'S YOUR PHONE. FROM JAPAN, I think!" Yun calls out from inside as she starts toward me with the phone. I am sitting in the shade on the balcony, sipping a glass of iced coffee.

I look at the display. "Caller information unavailable," it says. So Yun is right.

"Hurry! You must answer! It's your mother!" she prompts in an urgent tone.

Which is exactly why I don't want to answer. But reluctantly I do.

"Hello."

"Hiromi? What're you up to?" my mother says.

"Nothing in particular."

"This is Sunday. You have the day off. Aren't you going anywhere?"

"Nope."

"Guess what. I finally broke up with that guy. But now I feel so alone. All I can do is drown my sorrows."

"It's about time."

"You were right. It was a bad idea all along. Getting involved with a gambler."

"I wish you'd see that much on your own. Without me having to tell you."

"I guess I'm just not a good judge of character when it comes to men. This time, I'm through with them."

"Famous last words," I say with deliberate sarcasm.

"As I keep reminding myself, you really are all I have in the end. A complete stranger can't measure up to the child I carried inside my belly. After all, a parent and child have the same blood. When you're family, you have to help each other out. Sometimes I wonder what I raised you for."

I say nothing.

When I was the one in the weaker position—which is to say, when I was a child and she was the only person I had to depend on—she was never there for me. *I'm too tired,* she would say, turning a deaf ear to my pleas. *It's too much trouble.* And yet now that she's the weak one, she expects me to be there for her. If she thought she might want to lean on me someday, she should have given me a proper upbringing. Instead, she thinks she can just feed me, and then say, *I raised you, didn't I? Be grateful. Now take care of me.* Well, that's a bit much, if you ask me. Since I didn't go hungry, I'm not supposed to have any complaints? I'm not some domestic animal. It's not a special thing for a parent to feed her child; it goes without saying. Who else is supposed to do it? And yet she expects her child to spend the rest of her life repaying her with gratitude?

"Now that I'm all by myself," she goes on, "I just feel so lonely all the time. I cry a lot."

I'm still silent.

"I'd feel so much better if you were here in Japan."

"Well, I wouldn't feel better if I was in Japan."

"So when do you think you might come home?"

The woman is deaf to anything she doesn't want to hear. I don't know if she's deliberately ignoring me, or if it just automatically goes in one ear and out the other, but she's always been this way.

"I really couldn't say," I tell her.

"Really couldn't say? That's no answer. Next month? The month after?"

"Sorry, I have to go to the bathroom. These calls are expensive, so I'm going to hang up."

"Wait, wait! Do come home soon, dear. I'll be waiting for you. Call me."

"Yeah, yeah, yeah. Bye," I say quickly, and then hold down the button on my phone to turn it all the way off.

What am I waiting for? I should just remove myself from her family register and become a stranger to her. Disappear somewhere and end all possibility of her contacting me. But I've been contemplating that for more than ten years already, and I still can't bring myself to do it—which goes to show that I do feel indebted to her in some way. Memories of the days when it was truly a struggle for her just to put food on the table for me are etched deep into my being, and they've become an indelible part of me that cannot be wiped away.

I know my mother never meant me any harm. She was merely ignorant and uneducated and foolish, wanting in wisdom and knowledge.

Having noticed the icy tone of my responses, Yun asks, "You are not happy talking to your mother, Hiro?"

"We had a little fight," I say.

If I were to tell her how I truly feel about my mother, she'd probably look at me like I'm some kind of freak. The place her mother holds in her life is enormous and absolute.

I'M SURPRISED WHEN I GET A CALL FROM KONNO IN the middle of the day. I don't know what to say for a moment, but then he invites me out to dinner and joy floods through me. For longer than two months now, no matter when I call or text, his answer has always been that he's too busy, and I haven't been able to get anything else out of him. This must mean things have finally settled down for him a bit at work. I immediately feel the woman inside me growing restless. Konno is the one person right now who makes me feel like a woman. The eros between a man and a woman is uncomplicated, and brings me solace. The eros between two women is . . .

deep and amorphous, like a bottomless swamp, and fills me with misgivings.

We meet at the *izakaya*-style restaurant he took me to once before. I find him already there when I arrive, seated at a table in the corner. He's reading a newspaper over a beer, blending so well into his surroundings that I almost miss him.

"Hello," I say in a somewhat muted voice as I approach his table.

He lifts his eyes from the paper to look at me. "Long time no see," he says, curling his lips in an awkward smile. He folds the paper up small and sets it on the chair beside him.

As soon as I sit down a young waitress comes to ask what she can get me. She takes my order in a crisp, businesslike manner and soon returns with a mug of beer and the house appetizer. She eyes me without a smile as she places the two items on the table.

"So, how have you been?" he asks.

"Good, thanks. How about you? Looks like you've been getting some sun," I say, noticing his slightly darker complexion.

"Yeah. Playing golf."

"Golf in this heat sounds pretty dicey. I'd think you'd wind up with dehydration or heatstroke in no time."

"Yeah, I thought I'd die." The smile he gives me looks forced.

"You seem to be keeping busy."

"Pretty much, I guess. It's better than not having anything to do. I imagine you're keeping busy, too?"

"Things have been a bit quiet lately."

"Is that right?"

I don't answer. I can't help noticing that he's acting rather strangely. Saying very little. Avoiding my eyes. Behaving awkwardly. With an air of something weighing on his mind. A sense of foreboding grips my chest. My stomach tightens with dread, I can feel the tension pulling between my shoulders, and my agitation grows. I'm at sea in the oppressive silence.

Could it be he was never actually too busy to see me? Could it be he was deliberately avoiding me? That's the feeling I'm getting as I sit here right now, face to face with him. But if so, then why?

Has he grown tired of my willfulness, or perhaps lost patience with the way I've so coldheartedly kept him at arm's length? Is he on to my relationship with Yun—and repulsed by it? Or is it that he caught a glimpse of the darkness I hold inside me?

He keeps acting as if he has something he wants to say, but then he can't seem to make up his mind to do it and remains silent. Swigging his beer, nibbling on appetizers, he continues his search for the right moment to speak. When his mug is empty, the same waitress brings him another. She casts curious glances at him and looks as if she'd like to ask him something, but he seems determined not to notice and refuses to meet her eyes.

A customer across the room notices Konno and raises his hand in greeting. Konno bobs his head in return. The man stares at me as if he were looking at some exotic creature.

The restaurant is much more crowded now. When I first arrived, there was only a handful of customers, but now perhaps two thirds of the tables are filled. The diners are all Japanese men. The last time I came here, my reaction to this was merely one of surprise, but this time, the entire place rubs me the wrong way. Neither their beer nor their food is particularly good. The air-conditioning is cranked up too high and it's making me shiver. The man I saw drinking forlornly at the counter the other time is here again tonight, drinking by himself in exactly the same spot.

No matter how long I wait, Konno does not speak up. Has he changed his mind about what he was going to say? Is he thinking about saying good night without ever broaching what's on his mind? Running out of patience, I decide to take matters into my own hands.

"Is something going on?" I ask, doing the best I can to keep my voice calm.

"Huh? What do you mean?" He seems startled. I catch his eye for a moment, but he immediately shifts his gaze.

"You're not your usual self."

"Oh?"

"Look. You've obviously got something you want to tell me. You'll feel a lot better if you just come out and say it."

His eyes are fixed on the back of a customer at a table across the room.

"Don't worry about me. Are you looking for a way to let me down easy?"

I take in his appearance. Elbows propped on table, with hands clasped in front of chin. Collar of white shirt spread wide. Omega watch on wrist. Neatly trimmed nails. Big-boned, sturdy physique.

For several more moments he says nothing, as he seems to be considering something, but then he clears his throat and takes a deep breath. I wait for him to speak.

"We have kind of a funny relationship, don't you think? It's not like we're having some big romance. And we're not really even friends. But it also doesn't seem like it's a purely physical thing. Or am I the only one who thinks that?"

He's trying to make it sound spontaneous, but there's something forced in the way the words come out, like the lines spoken by a third-rate actor.

"No, I think that, too."

"I've never gotten the feeling that you really consider me your boyfriend."

For the first time this evening, he looks me straight in the eye.

"No, I guess not."

I return his gaze.

"Because your heart belongs to someone else."

What?

"Isn't that right?" he presses.

He has a look of utter assurance. What in the world is he trying to say?

"I'm sorry. What exactly are you getting at?"

I feel my face bunching up.

"Well, basically, I'm asking who your heart belongs to."

What an odd expression he has—smiling, yet somehow sad.

"Why would you be asking me something like that all of a sudden?"

"Because I'd like to know."

"Why do you want to know?"

"I wish you'd stop answering my questions with questions."

"Well, you don't consider me your girlfriend, either, right?" My voice rises, and takes on a contentious tone. I expected a simple, one-sided statement of some kind on his part and was listening in a completely passive frame of mind, so his abrupt question has me rattled. "In which case—"

"Wait. Stop," he says, abruptly raising his palm in front of my face to cut me off. "Let's not do this here. Let's go to my place." He quickly gulps down the rest of his beer. "Come on."

He rises to his feet and starts for the door. I hurry after him. The moment we're outside, my phone rings. It's Yun.

"Hi. Uh-huh. At the Japanese restaurant. That's right. I've already eaten. Uh-huh. All right, all right."

One thing I can count on when I'm out with Konno is that Yun will call. Every time, without fail.

"Was that Yun?" Konno asks after I click off. "Is she coming?" He sounds worried.

"No. I told her we're getting ready to leave," I say, and he heaves an audible sigh.

It's only about three minutes on foot from the restaurant to Konno's building. He briskly starts walking in that direction. I hand my ticket to the young parking attendant on duty outside, and he wheels my motorcycle out from the lot behind the building. After paying him, I straddle the bike and kick the starter. The engine fails to catch. I click my tongue. Down the street, I see Konno turn the corner and disappear. His building is on the left-hand side, only a short distance after rounding that corner. I really don't want to keep him waiting, but the engine won't catch. I kick the starter over and over without any luck, until finally the young man who retrieved my bike from the lot offers to help. He tries it once, and the engine immediately springs to life. When it comes to getting motorcycles started, Vietnamese men seem to have some kind of gift.

"*Cam on,*" I say, thanking him.

"You welcome," he answers in clumsy Japanese.

As I speed off, I wonder whether Konno will wait for me at the entrance to his building. I round the corner. I'm relieved to see him standing outside, but then I notice that he's not alone. There's someone else with him. Someone

much smaller. They are talking. Suddenly I realize that
the second person is Yun. I automatically let up on the
throttle. Yun? Why should Yun be here now? She didn't
say a word about being here a minute ago on the phone.
And yet there she is. My head spins. Konno sees me coming. Yun looks my way, too. I move slowly toward them,
as if pulled along by their two gazes.

Rolling to a stop, I dismount and stand in front of
them. Konno quickly averts his eyes, but Yun continues to
look at me.

"What are you doing here?" I ask.

"Waiting for you."

"What for?"

"To tell you important thing."

I figure she's simply up to her usual obstructionist
tricks. Any other time, I'd be a little irritated, but I'd take
it basically as a sign of how jealous she is, of how much
she loves me—and that would soothe me. Today, though,
I need to talk with Konno. I don't know what it's all about
yet, but it seems to be something very serious, so I really
can't let Yun interrupt us. If she gets in the way now,
Konno could lose the resolve he's finally mustered to
speak. I have to head her off.

"Can't it wait until tomorrow?" I say.

"No."

"All right. Tell me."

"Right here? It's not possible."

She glances toward Konno before she says this. He is
staring at the ground.

"Why does it have to be this minute? Why not when we had lunch today? Or yesterday. We had plenty of time then."

She doesn't answer right away. "It was difficult," she finally says.

"What was difficult?" I snap, glowering at her.

She mumbles something under her breath and falls silent. But then I see a sheepish smile spreading across her face. It annoys me, and I'm determined to get a clear answer.

"I asked—"

"You know what?" Konno cuts me off. "I can wait for another time. You go ahead with Yun now." He quickly steps toward the entrance as if he can't remove himself from the scene fast enough.

"Wait! I thought you had something to tell me. Isn't that why you wanted to see me, after all this time?"

"I'll call again," he says, and hurries through the door. Yun and I both gaze vacantly after him until he moves out of sight.

"Konno-san is gone," she says, with an expression that falls somewhere between a smile and a look of dismay.

"So are you happy? You got what you wanted. He's gone. Which means you can tell me now, right? What is it? What did you want to say?"

"You are angry."

"Yes, I'm angry. So tell me. What is it?

Yun averts her eyes. She makes no move to speak.

"Come on. Speak up."

"You are angry, so I not talk to you now."

Hearing her stock phrase makes my blood boil.

"Oh, so now you're suddenly going to clam up? I thought you were waiting here because you had to tell me something right this minute? What did you come for then?"

"It's okay."

"Huh?"

"I go home now."

She hops on her motorcycle parked nearby and starts up the engine.

"Wait, Yun! Hold on! Yun!" I yell as she ignores me and takes off down the street.

What is this? First Konno, and then Yun?

Now what do I do? I tilt my head back to look up at the building Konno lives in. Windows glow with light here and there, but it's not easy to tell which is his. After staring up at the luxurious façade for a time, I decide to give him a call. He doesn't answer. I had a feeling he wouldn't.

I ride around town on my motorcycle. It's after ten now. As I drive, I gradually begin to collect myself. Yun was supposed to cook dinner at my place tonight, but I told her I had a last minute date with Konno and canceled. That explains why she called when she did, exactly the way she always does. So far, everything makes sense. But then what? She turns out to be waiting for us in front of Konno's building. She's never done that before. She's come to meet me there and go home with me, but she's never waylaid me at the entrance like that. She said she had something to tell me. And it had to be right away. Thinking back on it now, I'd say she sounded a little desperate. Did she really have something to tell me? What could it be?

A motorcycle roars by me at breakneck speed. Yun once explained that the ones like that are pickpockets making a quick getaway. Why was I so sharp with her a while ago, I wonder regretfully.

I circle through town, round and round, turning the events of the evening over in my mind as I drive. But my thoughts just go round in circles, too, and I never arrive at any answers.

Near midnight I finally return to my apartment and crawl into bed, but my mind is alert and I cannot get to sleep.

I'M AWAKENED BY MY CHIRPY RINGTONE. THE ROOM is barely growing light. Thinking it must be Yun, I manage to get my sluggish brain going and pick up the phone.

"Hello?"

"Hiro! Yun's been in an accident!"

It's her little sister, Nhung. Her urgent voice jolts me wide awake and I leap out of bed.

"When? What happened?"

"She ran into a car. She's in the hospital."

"How bad is she hurt?"

"Can you come? Now?"

"I'll be there right away."

I take down directions and Yun's room number and hang up. It had to have happened on her way home last night, after she left me. I quickly throw on some clothes and hurry to the hospital.

When I arrive, I'm reassured to see that it's a large facility and relatively clean. It's worlds apart from the place where we went for Yun's hemorrhoidectomy. In the hallway, I stop a nurse to ask the way to the room.

It's a private room on the fifth floor. Yun is asleep when I enter. Nhung sits in an easy chair at the foot of the bed reading a magazine. She smiles when she sees me, and gets to her feet.

"She just went to sleep a little bit ago," she whispers, so as not to wake Yun.

"How bad is she hurt?"

"She broke her little toe. Otherwise she's just banged up—lots of scrapes and bruises. It happened at a corner when both vehicles were slowed down, so she didn't get hurt very badly."

"I see. That's good."

I gaze at the sleeping Yun from the foot of the bed. The sight of the gauze pad covering her left cheek gives me a wrenching feeling inside.

"Does she have to stay in the hospital?"

"Uh-huh. They want to keep her here at least for tonight—for observation. She's supposed to have nothing but bed rest for a while. The baby's fine for now, but I guess this is the time when they worry most about a miscarriage."

"Baby?"

I have no idea what Nhung is talking about.

"You know she's pregnant, right?"

"Pregnant?"

Her words are clear enough, but what they signify is so far outside the realm of imagination that I still cannot grasp their meaning.

"No way!" Nhung says, seeing the stupefied look on my face. "You didn't know either? They said she's in her third month."

Third month?

"Whose child is it?"

"Don't ask me. How should I know?"

"Did you know she was pregnant?"

"Uh-uh. I found out for the first time when the doctor told me a while ago."

"What did Yun say?"

"I haven't actually had a chance to talk to her about it yet. Anyway, I need a favor, Hiro. I have an important appointment to go to, so I need you to stay with her for a while. Is that okay? But just one thing. The baby's still a secret from the rest of the family, so you can't tell anybody about that yet, okay? No matter what."

"Okay," I say, nodding several times.

"I should be back around noon. See you then. Bye."

Nhung sweeps out of the room with her long chestnut hair flowing behind her. After pondering a few moments, I call Yamada to explain what's happened and ask for the day off.

Stepping to the bed, I peer down at Yun's face. She looks exhausted and appears to be sleeping deeply. I can hear the faint rise and fall of her breath. I carefully lift aside a lock of hair and press my palm softly against her forehead. It feels smooth and dry. Dropping to my knees, I slowly stroke my fingers through her hair.

"You know, I never had the slightest inkling," I whisper.

I twirl a lock of her hair with my forefinger.

"I guess you must be really good at keeping secrets."

I speak to her out loud as she continues to sleep.

"But I see now. . . . I finally see. . . . I think. Konno's the father, isn't he?"

There is no answer.

"Since when?"

My finger is still twirling, round and round.

"This has to be what you were both trying to tell me yesterday. Right? I mean, you were both acting so strangely. Last night."

Yun remains lost to the world.

"Maybe it's my own fault for not realizing. I'm pretty dense, I guess."

My finger twirls faster. Round and round and round and round.

What could I have been doing? I take my head in my hands and close my eyes. Part of me longs to hear the truth from Yun's own lips, while another part of me dreads it. After all, this is Yun with Konno we're talking about. How does that even happen? Yun and Konno . . .

really? Surely not. Surely it can't be Konno, can it? But if not him, then who?

I stare at the curve of the covers over Yun's belly. A new life is taking shape inside that belly. Within that tiny little body of hers is an even tinier living being. A living being that takes after Yun. A living being that draws nutrients from Yun's maternal body, and will look to her as protector and guardian. . . .

Wow.

Yun is going to be a parent.

She's going to be a mother.

The very same Yun?

Who's so like a child?

Who's so petite and cute?

It can't really be true, can it?

It has to be a lie.

Or some kind of mistake.

Doesn't it?

There's just no way.

No!

Absolutely not!

I don't want to see Yun become a mother.

Then Yun won't be Yun anymore.

She won't be my Yun.

My . . . Yun.

Whose Yun?

What are you talking about . . .

"My Yun"?

You know perfectly well nobody ever belongs to anybody else.
That's something you learned a long time ago.

What am I doing?

What could I have been doing?

The figure of Yun before me begins to fade. Her out-
lines grow blurry. She recedes into the distance.

The world we created between us—with its thick,
sultry air, and waves of sensuality only we could feel—
was like a bottomless black hole that sucked me into a
whole new universe. If only I could have stayed there.
If only I could have let myself be swallowed up completely into its deepest depths. What held me back, I
can only suppose, was the woman in me. I had lived my
whole life as a woman, when suddenly I fell in love with
another woman for the first time and lost my bearings
both in body and in soul. I didn't know how to make the
adjustment.

Intertwining our limbs and melding ourselves together, Yun and I built a world of our own that only we
knew. We all but became one, experiencing the same
things, thinking the same thoughts, and reaching out to
each other with the same needs. We understood this im-
plicitly. We were like attracted to like, like melting into
like, and it felt so right. My body responded in ways I'd
never experienced with a man. But it felt so unbelievably
good, so unbelievably amazing, that somewhere along
the way I grew uneasy. It was to dispel this uneasiness, I
now realize, that I began seeing Konno.

But realizing this now is simply too late. That universe

for just the two of us can no longer be attained, no matter how desperately I might yearn for it.

Without my ever noticing, Yun slipped quietly out of my arms. The seemingly boundless love she once had for me will now flow to Konno and their child, and only a few small dribbles will be left to come my way.

In the end, I simply loved her too much. I loved her more deeply than I could comprehend. And not knowing what to do with those feelings, frightened by them, I deceived myself by pretending not to notice how powerful they truly were.

Slowly rising to my feet, I leave Yun's hospital room.

I wheel my bike from the parking lot and set off down the street. Sunlight so intense it's like needles on my skin. Teeming masses of motorcycles. Cafés and food carts jamming the roadside. Signboards that glint brightly in the sun. Seeing the world around me the same as it ever was, I feel an agonizing tightness in my chest.

I always thought that Yun and I were alike. But I was wrong. It was a smug delusion. Yun was the mature one. After all, I'd be too scared to have a child. Which is not to say that I dislike children. Quite the opposite. It's because I love them that I shrink from having my own. I'm afraid I might become too attached to the child and make her unhappy. I'm afraid she might become my whole reason for living. I'm afraid I might smother her to death with my love. I'm afraid of what I'll do if I can't let her go. And most of all? I'm afraid that if blood tells, then my child will grow up to resent me, detest me, and shun me. Just as my grandmother did to her mother, my mother to hers, and I to mine.

Rooted in me, and giving shape to me, is my past—the past in which I was born of my mother, grew up in an insular country, and spent my days in the midst of that mysterious thing called society. Through the years, my skin has been penetrated by the indelible stains of that past, which cannot be removed by any brush, no matter how hard I might scrub; and attempting to paint them over with another color would create a thin mask that would peel away at the slightest rubbing.

Part of me changes day by day, and part of me remains the same. What will never change is the me of the past, when I lived in Japan.

I feel as though I've been left behind.

I have no idea what to do with the me that I've become.

I CIRCLE ABOUT THE CITY. FROM DISTRICT 5 THROUGH the center of District 1, and from there by way of District 3 to Phu Nhuan, Tan Binh, and District 10, back through Districts 5 and 1, across the bridge to Districts 4 and 7, and then back through District 4 to District 1.

More than three decades ago, Takeshi Kaiko said that Hondas are what make Saigon go round. Nothing has changed. To this day, it is Hondas that keep the city spinning. And this will no doubt remain true on into the future.

Garish Christmas-light displays. Houses decked in blinding arrays. Roadsides jammed with stalls selling gold and red Tet decorations. Yellow plum blossoms. Potted kumquat trees. Streets filled with Tet revelers. Countless gold-star-on-red flags waving in the breeze. The wildly rapturous crowds that resulted even in deaths when the Vietnamese team won an international soccer match. The always-busy juice bar selling black lotus-root drink. A disappointing soft-serve stand. My favorite bookstore. The restaurant where I ate frog-leg curry thinking it was chicken. The pricey café so famous among tourists where my sandwich was next to inedible. Events of every kind taking place in the parks. That frightening night in rapidly developing Saigon South. The crossing where I waited for the infrequent train to pass. Riding in waterproofs during the rainy season. The road along the river that stinks like a sewer but shines gloriously in the evening sun. The street where Nhung and Mai and Yun and I all crowded onto a single motorcycle and managed to keep our balance. The unlighted park that attracts both lovers and peepers at night. The Cambodian woman with reddish brown skin who sells incense at the temple gate. Believers on their way to the mosque. A Buddhist priest in his vestments speeding by on his scooter. The men who emerge at night to hawk adult DVDs on the street. Mountains of watermelons piled high in front of a store. The moon cakes sold everywhere for the Harvest Moon Festival. Early risers playing badminton in the park before it even grows light. City buses that think they own the roads and are forever getting into crashes. The frequent traffic jams that result. The street where I got rear-ended by a taxi cab. The rich man's son cruising the town in his luxury sedan. Singers in full stage dress rushing on motorcycles to their next gig. A grade-school boy engrossed in a comic book as he rides behind his mother. The massage parlor where a masseuse tried to give me a sensual massage. The house where Lam Truong lives. The tangy-sweet smell of the fruit market. The restaurant where we celebrated Yun's birthday. Getting lost in District 4 before I knew my way around. High-end motorcycles that are too big for their own good and get in everybody's way. The friendly lady with the infectious smile peddling embryonated duck eggs. The cheesy signboards at the movie theater betraying no flair for art. Pedestrians wearing sandals twelve months a year. Police enforcement mounted in the same spots every time. A broken-down motorbike being hauled on a cyclo. Blood running down a man's arm in the aftermath of an accident. A middle-aged battle-ax and a young gun yelling at each other after their bikes collide. A teenage girl on the verge of tears after a bike-borne thief snatches her necklace. Young punks hopped up on amphetamines driving wildly. The frequent blackouts that darken the city. A one-way street I always drove the wrong way on. The traffic law mandating rearview mirrors that sent everybody scurrying to buy them but caused so many accidents from tangled mirrors that it was quickly withdrawn. The constantly changing traffic laws, which therefore remain inscrutable. The ubiquitous motorcycle exhaust. Streets clouded with dust. Avenues that shimmer in the heat.

The swirling wind. The spinning city. The rich fertility of this land in the tropics, and the fathomless strength of the people who live in it.

I rode every one of these streets with Yun. I see her figure everywhere I turn. The sky was at times the bluest of blue, and the clouds blindingly white. The breeze after dark was always so refreshing.

Yun's bright smile represented so many precious things essential for living. Things like desire and hope. The smile of a southern land, radiant as the sun. The smile I so dearly, dearly love.

I drive endlessly about the city, on and on.

Round and round and round and round and round and round and round and round and round and round and round and round and round and round and round and round and round and round and round ...